DARK SILENCE

CHARLI CROSS SERIES: BOOK FIVE

MARY STONE

DONNA BERDEL

DESCRIPTION

Silence is the most terrifying scream...

When the beloved minister of a small inner-city church is killed in a drive-by shooting while delivering sandwiches to the homeless, Savannah Homicide Detective Charli Cross is on the case. Who would want to kill a man who does so much good? And why?

More importantly...was the pastor targeted or chosen at random?

While Charli and her partner, Detective Matthew Church, attempt to answer those questions, another shooting occurs...and then another. Soon, the town is terrified, and rightfully so. With each death, nothing will calm its citizens except catching the so-called "Savannah sniper" before he strikes again.

But how? With no links to connect the victims and no leads except for some grainy video footage and vague witness reports, they have no idea who his next victim will be, or when.

As the body count rises, Charli knows one thing for certain. There's nothing more dangerous than a killer with nothing to lose.

Suspenseful and unpredictable, Dark Silence is the fifth book in the Charli Cross Series from bestselling author Mary Stone and Donna Berdel. Think words are powerful? You might want to think again.

1

Victor Layne watched the night sky begin to lighten as the wheels of his bicycle spun against the pavement. Sunrise was only a few minutes away, and if he didn't hurry, he would miss it peeking over the Wilmington River.

Breathing in the cool air, Victor smiled. Now that it was officially autumn, the ambient air outside was getting a bit cooler, and it took longer for the sun to push away the chill from the previous night. Not that a low of sixty was cool—this was Savannah, Georgia after all—but it sure was a contrast to the mid-eighties they still experienced during the day.

Nothing could hinder Victor from his morning routine, though, and even when fall turned into winter, he bundled up and stuck to his route. There were people who depended on him.

In his younger years, he never missed a morning jog, not even on the coldest days. Back then, Victor had relished the feeling of the chilly air searing his lungs with every breath. There was nothing quite like communing with the great outdoors at the start of every day.

Now in his mid-sixties, Victor had a hard time walking long distances with his bad knees, let alone running. When his joints had begun to wear out, he traded his daily jogs for bike rides. Since the doctor recommended—even insisted—that he continue to exercise every day, just at an easier pace, these daily jaunts kept his heart healthy.

Victor hadn't just obliged his physician's advice, he was glad for it. Riding his bike let him cover even more ground, allowing him to deliver his wife's daily basket of sandwiches to the homeless and needy while still getting his exercise. He would start in his neighborhood and venture out to some rougher areas, ending his route at the river to watch the sun rise and pray before pedaling back home.

Stopping at a familiar alley, Victor climbed off his bike and grabbed the last bag from the basket. This one was marked with a D, and he'd been saving it for this last—and favorite—visit.

"Henry?" Victor peered into the darkness of the alley and got a little *ruff* in return. Cans and other debris rattled before a skinny man with long silver-streaked hair lumbered into the light, a dog at his side.

"Mornin', Pastor Layne." Henry still wore the tattered camouflage jacket he'd been given before being sent to Afghanistan twenty years ago. Beside him, the lab mix wagged his tail furiously.

Though his knees popped and groaned, Victor knelt to pet the animal and got a sloppy lick up his cheek in return. "Hungry, Freedom?"

He loved the dog's name. Victor just wished the mind of the canine's owner would be free from the trauma that had haunted him for so long. During one of Victor's visits with Henry, the vet told him he only felt safe behind a dumpster "that no bullet could go through."

It was so very, very sad.

To make things worse, Animal Control had attempted to take Freedom away from Henry several times, stating that the emotionally disturbed vet couldn't possibly care for the dog while on the streets. To them, euthanasia was a better option. They didn't stop hounding Henry until Victor stepped in, promising to deliver the pair a daily meal.

It was just one of the reasons Victor refused to miss a single day.

Pulling a plastic bag filled with two cups of kibble and a large can of wet dog food from the paper bag, Victor smiled as the dog's tongue lolled out, a huge grin spreading across his furry face.

"Something for you." Victor handed the remaining contents to Henry. "And something for you." Digging into his pocket, Victor pulled a dog biscuit out. "And a little treat too."

Freedom practically vibrated at the sight, but he was much too well mannered to jump for the bone. He was a good dog, cared for by a good man the world had turned its back on.

Henry lifted a plastic bowl Victor had bought for the dog about a year ago. "Thank ya kindly, Pastor Layne. Tell the preacher 'thank you', Free."

As though he was in front of a king, Freedom lowered his head in a regal bow. It always made Victor smile and lower his torso in return. "You are very welcome, Master Freedom."

Victor emptied the contents into the bowl Henry held, placing the treat on top like a cherry on a bowl of ice cream. With another heartfelt "thank you," the pair retreated back into the shadows to enjoy their meal.

Still smiling, Victor climbed on his bike and pedaled away. The smile faded, though, as he was forced to navigate around a few bags of trash. The area was getting worse. Just like Victor's own neighborhood.

As much as he tried to help, his community was in steady

decline. When he'd bought his home decades ago, it had been a wonderful area for families. Over the years, Victor had witnessed many of the children on his street grow up, walking to and from school each day and playing outside every evening until their mothers called them to come inside and eat dinner. Those children had long since transitioned into adults and now had families of their own, most of whom had moved away.

BE CAREFUL.

Tiny hairs stood on the back of Victor's neck as the words whispered through his brain. Where they had come from wasn't a question that sprang to Victor's mind...he knew they were from God and trusted the caution.

But caution from what?

He glanced around, seeing nothing.

Although Victor's own neighborhood was going downhill and his bike route was in an even rougher part of Savannah, he wasn't afraid. Not usually. Everyone in the area knew him, and he believed everyone was a child of God, regardless of their circumstance.

Truth be told, though, Victor also knew he was no longer a spry young man. His age was a blanket of vulnerability that he had to wrap himself in at all times, but one thing was certain. He would continue to stay as healthy as possible for as long as he could.

His daily bike route was part of what kept Victor strong, both physically and mentally. Just being outdoors provided inspiration as he brainstormed for his weekly sermons. He had been a minister for nearly forty years. After getting his Master of Divinity at the Candler School of Theology, he took a position at a small congregation in Savannah.

From that very first day at Cornerstone Presbyterian,

Victor had known he wanted to spend his life working at this church. And oh, what a first day it was. Moving to the sidewalk on the left side of the street, he pedaled a bit harder, ensuring he didn't slack off on his pace as his mind wandered. The memories of that first Sunday with his new congregation were so vivid in his mind, it could have been yesterday.

Over the years, he'd met other ministers who were so driven by their egos that they craved the power the ministry provided them. They were always looking to work in more prestigious churches, to minister to more people.

But that was never what Victor wanted. His only desire was to help a local community, as he believed with certainty that one minister was doing far more important work when he could connect with every member of his church. And he had done exactly that.

Pastor Layne—as many of his congregation called him— knew every face, was aware of every challenge they endured. From addiction to marital issues to the loss of a loved one, Victor walked through life side by side with each member.

Although he loved the members of his church—the younger ones like they were his own children—Victor had never had kids of his own. Truth be told, he had once entertained the idea that he might meet a good Christian woman and raise a family. But Victor followed God's calling for him in every step of his life, and God never called him to have children, even after meeting his beautiful wife. At times, he longed to be surrounded by blonde-haired, blue-eyed children—he was certain his offspring would favor his wife—but for the most part, he was content to serve where God had called him.

"My congregation is the only child I need."

As his mind wandered back to the people who would be watching him from their wooden benches, Victor slowed his pedaling and went over his Sunday sermon in his head. His knees may have given out over the years, but his mind never did. Still sharp as a whip, he was able to memorize an entire sermon without ever needing to write it down.

Perhaps that came from many years of working as a minister. When someone did something week by week, they were bound to become skilled at it. And Victor was certainly skilled at crafting his sermons without taking notes.

"As God's love for us persists, so shall the love we feel for our neighbors." The words flowed from his lips as he pedaled toward the river. The water was in sight now. "And who are our neighbors? Everyone we come in contact with. Not just those in our social circles, but the downtrodden, those who have not been fortunate to experience the blessings we have in our lives." Victor nodded to himself, pleased with what he would preach this coming Sunday.

The sermon was just as much for Victor as it was for his congregation. Although he encountered homeless people daily, he reminded himself often that they were equally as important to God as anyone else. After all, God didn't pass judgment on these people, and neither should he.

Be careful.

For the second time that morning, tiny hairs stood to attention. This time, though he glanced around and didn't spot an immediate threat, he had the unmistakable feeling that he was being watched. Forcing himself to be discreet, he glanced more fully over his right shoulder.

It was only a car.

Whew.

Sweet relief swept through him, and he expelled the breath growing stale inside his lungs. Why had he gotten so nervous? He delivered food to the homeless every day, and he'd never been afraid to bike through the area.

With a hearty chuckle, Victor mentally chided himself for

being so on edge. Hadn't he just been reviewing his sermon about loving his neighbors? Speaking of which...

He scolded himself for not being more attentive to the newcomers in his own neighborhood in recent years. As soon as he got home, he would ask his wife to bake a pie for a couple across the street who had just moved into the house a few weeks prior. They would invite the young family over for coffee and dessert.

Maybe that was why he was feeling so on edge. He was being cautioned by God to not forget the neighbors close to him while he cared for those farther away.

Yes. That must be it.

A smile played across Victor's lips as he drew nearer to the river. He began to slow his pace as the soft glow of twilight surrounded him. Once he reached the water, he'd get off his bike and sit on a bench to watch the sun rise and pray.

Should I ask Lydia to make an apple pie or a blueberry one? Or maybe blackberry cobbler and homemade vanilla ice cream?

A cough brought Victor back to reality, and he glanced over his shoulder again. The car was closer now, but not close enough for him to make out the driver.

Why was it going so slow?

Was the driver following him?

He shook his head and continued to pedal down the empty sidewalk, forcing himself to think logically. *I'm being ridiculous. They're probably just enjoying a quiet morning drive in the area as they head to work.* Victor began to recite his sermon out loud again, forcing himself to dispel any fear attempting to creep into his mind.

It worked for a moment. When his attention waned, Victor reminded himself of his congregation and his devotion to the Lord's work, tapping into his sense of inner peace.

The car's engine grew louder, and the hair on Victor's

neck rose again. A quick glance over his shoulder told him what he already knew. The car was closer now. His body may be slowing down these days, but his hearing was still dead on.

Don't panic. It's just a fellow human being, one who needs the love of God just like everyone else.

He chanced another glance at the silvery gray car, but couldn't see past the glare of the streetlights reflecting off the front window.

Determined to calm his racing heart, Victor willed himself to take slow, steady breaths and started to recite one of his favorite chapters from the Bible as he pedaled harder. "The Lord is my shepherd..."

He let out a shaky breath, the scripture that was usually like a soothing balm failing to calm his trembling nerves. "I shall not want."

In that moment, Victor swore he could hear the voice of God Himself in his ear, except God wasn't leading him beside still waters. Instead, the voice seemed to say, *"Pedal faster, Victor! Pedal as fast as you can, and don't look back!"*

As if he'd been jolted by a prod, Victor didn't have to be told twice to listen to the booming voice of God. Arthritis or not, he was getting out of dodge. His black sweats slid up his legs as he pedaled as hard and as fast as he could. Victor took in deep, heaving breaths as his bad knees protested. It had been a long time since he'd forced himself to pedal this hard, and his calves burned in protest.

The car was beside him now.

He didn't dare glance over and make eye contact with the driver, though not making eye contact was hardly going to be enough to keep him safe. If the man had wanted anything mundane, like to ask for directions, he would have asked already. There was something menacing about this person's intentions, and God was telling Victor as much.

After decades in the church, Victor knew how to hear His word. And He made it clear that Victor was in imminent danger.

Why?

Victor had no money on him. Even all his sandwiches were gone. The bike he rode had been used when he purchased it and couldn't be worth more than fifty dollars.

It's not money they want.

A chill ran down his spine at the thought. As Victor struggled to keep a steady pace, his sweet wife rushed through his mind. He had to get home to her. She'd been baking a pound cake in preparation for her sister's visit and had promised Victor a slice when he returned. Victor had to taste that cake. He had to see the face of his wife once again. But a nauseating turn in his stomach told him a simple truth...he might not.

When he was just yards away from the banks of the river, his mind scurried for a plan. He might be able to force his bike off the sidewalk and down to the river's edge.

And break your neck in the process?

Maybe he could just hide behind some nearby bushes, and the guy would leave. There were normally quite a few people walking or jogging by the river each morning. The driver would have to exit his vehicle and search to find him and wouldn't want to be seen. Most petty criminals wouldn't be bothered to go that far for a robbery, right? Why would someone be following Victor if not to rob him?

When the car crossed the center line and began driving on the left side of the street, Victor gave one last hard pedal as he reached a wall of azaleas. He was ready to hop off his bike and duck into the bushes when a voice stopped him.

"Hey, Pastor Layne! Can we talk?"

And just like that, the tension rolled off his body in waves. This was someone who clearly knew him. And if Victor wasn't mistaken, the voice was familiar, though the owner's name momentarily fled his mind.

I'm a moron.

Victor chastised himself for not being open to the possibility that someone he knew might be flagging him down. After all, he had hundreds of members in his congregation. At any time, one could see him riding his bike and stop by to say hello.

But why had the driver taken so long? Maybe he'd been on a phone call and was waiting until it ended?

Victor shook his head, dismissing all the questions bouncing inside his noggin. He was worrying over nothing.

Releasing a long breath, he climbed off his bike and shoved the kickstand down with a foot. "My, oh my. You have no idea how much you scared this old man." Placing a trembling hand over his pounding heart, Victor willed his brain to produce a name. "So good to see you...son." He leaned down to see the driver's face better. "I hope you're doing well."

Victor was expecting the man's expression to light up in response.

It didn't.

From the darkness within the interior of the vehicle, solemn eyes stared back at him from a face as emotionless as death.

Victor wiped at the sweat forming on his brow, flashing a tentative smile. "Is everything okay?"

The black barrel of a gun was his only response.

Taking a step back, Victor had only an instant to realize that this wasn't a friendly visit before he bumped into his bicycle. In a tangle of metal, he and the bike struck the asphalt hard.

God had been right in His warning to run, but had Victor listened? No.

From the ground, Victor held out both hands, as if the bones and flesh could shield him from a bullet. "Son..." Why couldn't he think of this man's name? "What do you want?"

The gun moved past the driver's side window, and the corner of his assailant's mouth quirked up on one side. "How's your faith protecting you now, Pastor Layne?"

And just like that, Victor understood.

He'd failed this man in some significant way. But how?

The question didn't even matter because Victor saw the truth in his assailant's dead eyes. There would be no talking his way out of this. Instead of trying, Victor attempted to untangle himself from the bike as he began to finish his earlier prayer.

"Even though I walk through the valley of the shadow of death..." Victor had read this same scripture over many a deathbed and funeral. The words poured from his mouth as easily as water from a glass. "I will fear no evil, for you are with me."

But Victor was afraid. Very.

As the rest of the words stumbled from his lips, images of his wife flashed through his mind. What would happen to the homeless people who relied on him for food each day? His congregation? To Freedom?

He had so much left to do on this Earth.

The man Victor couldn't name smiled, even wider this time, as his finger moved to the trigger.

"And I will dwell in the house of the Lord for—"

Bam!

2

C haos.

It was the only word Detective Charlotte Cross could use to describe the horde of people standing past a line of police cars near the Wilmington River. Lookie-loos had their phones out, attempting to record the hustle and bustle of the bloody crime scene.

Charli would never understand the fascination people had with trauma. If she wasn't working and happened to drive by an obvious crime scene, she wouldn't just stop and stare. She would stop to see if she could be of assistance, but that was a far cry from gawking for her own entertainment.

Sadly, that was the way many people reacted in an emergency situation, when the likelihood of at least one out of four or more people stopping to help rather than stare was only thirty-one percent. These people were vultures, no doubt trying to see how many likes they could get for their videos on social media.

But Charli did her best to ignore the onlookers around the perimeter as she and Detective Matthew Church, her partner in the Savannah Police Department, walked up to an officer standing over a sheet-covered body.

Matthew visibly shuddered as they turned to the officer in charge of the scene and signed their information into the logbook. Knowing how badly her partner detested being around murder victims, Charli took the lead. "May we see?"

The officer lifted the sheet just enough for the detectives to get a glimpse of the body. Although Charli couldn't tell how many shots had been fired, there were bullet wounds in the victim's head and chest.

"Thanks." Charli nodded for him to re-cover the poor soul. "What can you tell us?"

Officer Brian Anderson glanced at a couple of other beat cops who were several yards away, each standing next to a bystander. "Meet Victor Layne. Appears he was shot by a driver in a gray or silver Honda. We've got two witnesses, and before you ask…" the officer held up a hand as Charli opened her mouth, "yes, we kept them separated. They're both pretty shaken up, but they're ready to answer questions."

Nodding her approval, Charli scanned the area before turning back around to face the officer. "How do we know it was the driver and not a passenger?"

"According to the witness testimony," Anderson glanced down at the notes he'd taken, "there was only one person in the car."

Charli reached for the papers Anderson extended before Matthew could snatch them up. Her partner was dependable, but she liked to make sure she got all the details firsthand. "No model on that gray slash silver Honda?"

Anderson removed his hat and ran a finger through his blond hair as he sighed, though it was cut too short for his fingers to cause any movement of the follicles. "Unfortunately, it appears neither of our witnesses got a great view of the model since it was just getting daylight when the shooting happened. They both admit to only seeing the word 'Honda.' They can't identify it any more than that."

Matthew swiped the back of his hand across the beads of sweat that had formed on his forehead. "Maybe if we show them different models, they'll be able to identify it that way."

The twenty-something officer grinned at Matthew, and Charli could have sworn the beat cop puffed out his chest a little. "I tried to show them different models, but according to them, the car was a beater. And once I started showing them Hondas from the nineties, neither one was able to tell one from the other. One of the witnesses said the cars all looked the same to them. I don't think you're going to have much luck with that."

Well, that was disappointing. Knowing the model would have been immensely helpful in finding registered owners. Honda was an extremely common car make, especially if the car was potentially over a decade old. Although the list of gray or silver Hondas in Savannah would be endless, at least this was a start.

Charli finished jotting down a note to check out nearby cameras and handed the young officer's papers back to him. "Thank you, Officer."

One of the witnesses was sitting on one of the many stone benches overlooking a playground near the river. Poor girl couldn't have been older than fifteen. Her gray Groves High School sweatshirt wrinkled at the bottom where it touched her tattered jeans. Whether these rips were made from wear or were designed to look old, Charli couldn't tell. But the girl was picking at a hole where loose fabric strings hung down on the denim, her face the very definition of nervous.

Charli did her best to plaster her most sympathetic look on her face as they approached. "Hello, I'm Detective Cross, and this is my partner, Detective Church. We want to talk to you about what you saw here today." Charli glanced over at Matthew. He had on his fatherly smile, which was sure to help put the young woman at ease.

The teenager gazed down at her feet. "I'm Selena Hine. I...I didn't really see much. I'm sorry." There was a stutter in her voice, and she appeared to be perilously close to tears.

"No need to apologize." Not wanting to hover over the teenager, Charli took a seat on the bench. Maybe that would help put her at ease. "What was your reason for coming to the river today?"

"Well, I was walking to school, and this is on my way. Sometimes, I sit on one of the benches for a bit and enjoy the quiet if I have a few minutes to spare, but I was running late this morning."

Charli glanced at her watch. The shooting had happened at approximately five after seven. "Late? Isn't seven early for classes to begin?"

Selena pulled at another thread on her jeans. "I was supposed to be at school at seven for a study group, so I was practically running to get there. I stopped here to fill up my bottle at the fountain. I was looking down at my water bottle right over there when it happened." She pointed at a fountain about fifteen feet to the right. "I wasn't very far away, maybe about thirty or forty feet...and it was so loud." She swiped a hand under her nose. "I thought someone had set off a firework or something. My water bottle fell when I jumped."

Matthew sat down on the other side of Selena, taking Charli's lead. "What happened next?"

"I turned around just for a second, and I saw someone on the ground." Selena drew in a deep, shuddering breath before tucking her hair behind her ears. "He was on top of a bicycle, so I thought he'd just fallen off it. But..." She swallowed hard. "It was just...all red from the blood on his face and chest.

And this gray car was right next to him. It stayed there for a second, but then it drove off real fast after. So fast, there was this loud screeching sound from the tires."

Selena's eyes were as big as saucers, but the expression on her face was blank. In Charli's experience, it wasn't uncommon for a witness in shock to display minimal emotional expressions.

Matthew shifted on the bench. "What else can you tell us about the car?"

"I saw the word "Honda" on the back." Selena picked up a dented water bottle and took her time unscrewing the lid. "But like I told the other police officer, I don't know much about cars. I'm really sorry."

Charli flashed her a soft smile and continued with a gentle tone. "That's okay, Selena. But was there anything else you noticed about the car?"

Taking a long, slow drink from the bottle, Selena fumbled with the lid, her hands shaking. "It was scratched all over, but I can't think of where the scratches were exactly. The car moved away so fast after I heard the shot, and I hadn't even noticed it before then. I just know it wasn't in good condition."

Though the officer had already told them that the witness had only seen one person in the vehicle, Charli wanted to double check. "How many people were in the car?"

Selena pressed her fingertips to her temple. "Just one, I think. But I'm not one hundred percent sure about that. I just know I only saw the shadow of one head."

"What can you tell us about the driver?" Matthew leaned forward, his elbows resting on his knees. It was the kind of relaxed, casual stance that would help the witness not feel too much pressure about her testimony.

"I couldn't see them at all. The back windows were all dusty. I wish I knew more. I couldn't even get the license plate. There was something black over it. Or maybe it was blue." Selena's lip began to quiver, and she pushed aside her blonde sideswept bangs cascading over her eyes. "I think it was some kind of fabric. Maybe I should have run over to the person after they got shot, but I..." Tears dropped from her chin. "I couldn't move."

This poor girl.

"That's completely normal, Selena." Though Charli loathed most human contact, she found herself reaching for the girl's hand. "You have nothing to feel bad about. I'm sure that was quite a shock."

Watching this fifteen-year-old so devastated as she tried to piece together the events for the police, Charli's mind wandered to a younger version of herself after the kidnapping of her best friend Madeline. Charli had been a little older than Selena, but her reaction was similar. The guilt of not doing more when Madeline was taken had surged through her. And she certainly didn't want this young woman to experience the same feeling.

Of course, Charli's words seemed to fall on deaf ears. Selena was just too shaken to absorb what Charli was telling her.

Charli suppressed a sigh. Maybe later on, Selena would recall bits and pieces of this conversation. "We call this the fight, flight, or freeze reaction. When faced with a traumatic event, many people will either respond by fleeing the scene or being frozen in place. I promise it's a normal reaction. You did nothing wrong."

Selena nodded wordlessly. Dark, empty eyes stared off into the distance. From her own experience, Charli had no doubt the witness would remember this traumatic event for the rest of her life.

"Is there anything else you can remember about the car or scene? Anything at all we should know?" Charli forced herself to put her concern for Selena aside and gather as much information as possible.

Selena only shook her head, biting her lower lip.

Matthew stood and rubbed his lower back. "Have you called your parents yet?"

"Yes, sir, my mom is coming to get me as soon as she can leave work. She's waiting for her replacement now. She's a nurse, so she can't just leave."

"That's no problem at all." Matthew smiled down at her. "Your mom is doing important work. Once she gets here, we'd like to get her permission to speak with you again later on at the precinct. Meanwhile, our officer is going to sit with you until she arrives, all right?"

Selena nodded, and Charli felt a twinge of guilt for leaving her alone to interview the other witness. But the girl didn't seem to mind. And Charli could relate to that because she, too, didn't like to talk while processing trauma.

The other witness was a thirty-five-year-old father. Leon Rodriguez lived just down the block and had been outside on his front porch waiting for his ex-wife to drop off their children so he could take the kids to school. It was their usual schedule since the ex had to be at work much earlier than he did. Right after calling 9-1-1 about the shooting, he told his ex-wife not to bring the kids but to go ahead and take them to school.

But Leon echoed the same experience Selena had. The car was too dirty to get a view through the back windows, and Leon wasn't close enough to the front of the car to see through the open window. Nevertheless, he was confident the shot came from that car, as nobody else was even close. He was able to identify a dent in the left side of the bumper, a detail that Selena hadn't remembered.

The detectives collected both Leon and Selena's contact information and gave their own numbers in case they remembered more details later. By the time they'd finished up, the crime scene techs had arrived and were setting up a screen around the body so the lookie-loos wouldn't be able to view what was going on.

Charli made her way back to Officer Anderson. "Have we got any next of kin to inform?"

"Someone is already on their way to speak with his wife. I found out the victim was a minister at Cornerstone Presbyterian." Officer Anderson leaned against his squad car, looking weary to his core.

Charli pulled her small notebook out of her blazer to jot down the information. "A minister, huh? Not the usual type to be a victim of a drive-by."

Anderson folded his arms. "I know, right? Don't know what to make of it. The man has no priors. If he was involved in any illegal activity, we don't know about it."

Matthew turned toward Charli. "It could be completely random. Some gang initiations require a random shooting to join."

Charli tucked her notebook and pen back into her pocket. "Possibly. Maybe they thought if they killed a random bystander, they'd be less likely to get caught."

If that was what happened, the perp would be right about that. Not only were random crimes the ones that most often went unsolved, but those done in a city where the offender didn't reside added yet another layer of stealth. In many cases, motive led detectives to the perpetrator. If there wasn't a clear motive, this case would be hard to solve.

But Charli didn't know nearly enough about this case yet to assume it was gang related. The minister might not be involved in any past criminal activity, but that didn't mean he had no enemies. Hell, sometimes those who appeared to be the most exemplary citizens were involved in the most heinous crimes, a fact that Charli's experience as a detective had taught her all too well.

That wasn't always the case, of course. But Charli had learned that she couldn't always take people at face value. She had to dive into someone's life before she made any decisions about a potential perp.

As Matthew chatted with the officer, Charli only half-listened as she explored all avenues for learning about the personal life of this minister. They could speak to his wife, to members of his church...she ran through the possibilities in her head. But as she did, she spotted a gas station across the street. It was at least fifty yards away, but maybe...

"Hey, Officer Anderson. Have we asked yet if they have any CCTV footage?"

A bit of red flushed Anderson's cheeks. Charli assumed that was a no, and he was embarrassed that he hadn't approached the store already. "Uh, I don't think we have, unless one of the other officers forgot to tell me."

Charli nodded. "I guess we know where we're going first."

3

Charli perused the cluttered gas station and liquor store combo. Muddy footprints littered the once white tile floors. The place was a total mess, even for an area as undesirable as this one.

On top of being filthy, the gas station had a lot of wear and tear. Paint was chipping off the white wooden shelving units. To locate the lotto scratchers available at the front of the store, someone would have to be able to see through glass that was scratched to high heaven.

Stepping over a candy bar wrapper, Charli frowned. She didn't expect too much from this neighborhood, but this was beyond the pale for a business establishment. The houses were older and a bit run-down, but most residents did the best they could.

In Savannah, old neighborhoods could go one of two ways. Either they became historical hot spots with very expensive, highly coveted homes, or they fell into disarray. And this neighborhood certainly wasn't a hot spot for anything good.

"Hello?" Matthew put both hands around his mouth and bellowed, trying to get someone's attention.

Since it was morning and the "open" sign was mostly lit up, surely someone had to be present. But even with Matthew hollering, nobody came.

Matthew made his way over to one of the snack aisles, leaning over a row of candy bars.

Charli tapped her foot, shooting her partner a look of impatience. "What are you doing?"

He shrugged, giving her a sheepish grin. "I'm grabbing a snack. Might as well if we're going to be stuck here."

Seriously?

"Stuck here?" She forced herself not to smile at her partner. "Matt, we entered two minutes ago. It's a gas station, not *Gilligan's Island.* I don't think you're going to be stranded here until you're old enough to retire."

He held up a candy bar before waltzing over to the front counter and tossing it down. "Hey, I need my energy. It's not like we always get to eat regular meals at this job."

Charli was in the middle of rolling her eyes when an employee finally walked out from the back. The name tag "Austin" was pinned at the chest of a man in his early twenties whose blue eyes were a stark contrast to the bloodshot sclera. A dank smell followed him, wafting out of the back room. No doubt he didn't hear the detectives because he was out back with a joint. Charli knew that glazed look when she saw it, but she wasn't here to catch a young man for pot. She had a murder to solve.

"Can I help you?" The words were slow to roll off Austin's tongue, taking many more seconds than necessary.

Charli choked back a cough. "Hi, yes. I'm Detective Cross, and this is my partner, Detective Church. We need to know if this business has any security footage."

Now aware he was standing in front of two detectives,

Austin stood up straight. His eyes widened, a common move for people under the influence of marijuana. Maybe people thought it made them look more awake and less high. But most of the time, that wide-eyed look only made them appear paranoid. And in Austin's case, it made the redness much more obvious.

"Why?" This time, Austin's question didn't come out slow. It practically flew out of his mouth. He began to smooth out his wrinkled shirt. *Just give up, buddy. There's no hope for those wrinkles.* "What are you looking for?"

Charli didn't want him to think they cared about his marijuana usage. If he even remotely believed there was a chance the cops were there for him, he'd be more resistant to showing them security footage. "Did you happen to hear any unusual noises outside earlier this morning?"

"Fireworks, you mean? Kids mess with them all the time around here. Why?" Austin continued to glance between Charli and Matthew, reminding her of one of those black Kit-Cat Klocks from the thirties. Charli's grandma used to keep one in the living room.

Matthew fiddled with the candy bar he'd tossed on the counter. "That wasn't a firework. It was a gunshot. And we need to see if any important footage was attained by your security cameras out front. Are they in working condition?"

Every previously tensed muscle in Austin's body seemed to release when he realized the detectives hadn't come to arrest him for weed. Charli hid a smirk. If they weren't in such a hurry, she might find the situation a little more amusing.

The young man shoved his hands in his pockets and knitted his brows. "Wait, was anyone hurt?"

Charli hated interviewing individuals who were high since it was difficult for them to stay focused. "We're not at liberty to discuss the details of this case. But we do need access to your security footage."

"Oh, uh, I don't know if I'm allowed." Austin leaned against the glass shelving behind the counter that held the liquor. "See, my manager doesn't like to share our security footage with anyone."

Matthew leaned his elbows against the countertop, cupping his chin in his hands. "Not even with the police?"

Austin ran a hand through his long, unkempt hair. Locks of his wavy hair went in every direction. Charli doubted he'd brushed it all week. Between his messy hair and a wrinkled shirt that sported more than a day's worth of stains, she surmised that personal hygiene wasn't a big priority for this young man.

"Especially cops, actually. I mean, look at the neighborhood, man." He waved a hand at the direction of the window. "We don't want to be targeted because we're sharing video footage with the cops. It's not our job to police what people do outside our doors."

"Hmm." Charli tapped a finger against the glass counter next to the cash register. "I suppose your boss is entitled to his feelings. Though I am curious how he feels about you smoking weed during work hours."

Charli kept her voice light. She didn't want to threaten the kid, just unnerve him a little. If they had to get a warrant to come back and access the security footage, it would slow down their progress on the case. Walking out with that footage right away was ideal.

"What?" Austin swallowed hard. "I dunno what you're talking about."

"Oh, come on, Austin." Matthew gave a dramatic shake of his head. "You smell like you just got into a fight with a skunk."

Austin sucked air between his teeth. "All right, whatever.

Screw it. I don't care if you have the footage but hurry up. I don't want anyone to see you."

The live camera footage from three cameras was sitting on a monitor on a beat-up metal desk in the office. But to Charli's disappointment, the images were pretty grainy. She hoped when they rewound the footage, the images would be a little clearer.

Unfortunately, that wasn't the case. Going back to earlier in the morning, Charli and Matthew watched until a man riding a bike down the sidewalk appeared in the top left section of the screen. The cyclist looked over his shoulder and then began pedaling again. Faster this time? It sure seemed so, but that didn't necessarily mean anything sinister.

Seconds later, a sedan crossed the center lane and pulled up next to him, going the wrong way. Squinting hard, Charli thought it very well had the body shape of a Honda, but it was a pixilated blur. If Charli didn't already know the model from the witness testimony, she wouldn't be able to tell from this footage. She certainly couldn't make out a face through the vehicle's windows, and she also couldn't tell for sure how many people were in the car.

Even the victim was hard to make out, but at least the camera was set at an angle that gave Matthew and Charli some visibility of him stopping the bike. Just over the top of the vehicle, they watched the victim turn toward the car.

Matthew leaned in closer. "You think he knew the driver?"

Charli's nose was practically touching the screen. "Maybe. The person in the car might have flagged him down. They could've said they needed directions or something. Why would he be suspicious of a random car to begin with? No real reason not to approach this car."

If a stranger flagged her down for directions, she

wouldn't give it a second thought. She'd been asked about directions many times before.

Matthew sat on the rickety metal chair in front of the monitor. "No, I think he was suspicious. Look, it's hard to see, but if we rewind here, he glances over his shoulder and then sped up just before the car pulled next to him."

Matthew was right. The victim had absolutely started pedaling faster.

Charli was just about to curse the lack of audio when Victor Layne lifted his hands and took a step back. A second later, his arms pinwheeled and he tumbled out of sight.

Was that the moment he'd been shot? It certainly looked that way from the video. Then why did the vehicle linger for many seconds longer?

She glanced at Matthew, knowing he was fighting the urge to look away from the footage. No matter how many times they had witnessed death, seeing the moment a life was stolen from someone never got any easier. Knowing that some heartless monster had taken a person away from his loved ones would always be a knife to their hearts.

For a moment, Matthew shared her silence. Aware that her partner struggled with watching death more than she did, Charli was able to compartmentalize what was happening and view it more objectively. It wasn't that she was heartless, but she preferred to turn off her emotions as much as she could while figuring out the details of a case.

The car drove away, just as the witnesses said it had. The minister was left on the ground, likely dead the moment he was shot. Charli wouldn't need a medical examiner to tell her that much. He'd been shot in the head and the chest.

Charli sighed, her heart heavy. "We should go to every business in this area that may have security cameras. Maybe we can see where he made his next turn and follow him that way. And let's have a couple officers canvass the neighborhood to see if anyone had a doorbell camera nearby." Charli wasn't too hopeful about that, though, considering this was a low-income area. They were far more prevalent in wealthier neighborhoods.

They'd already put out an APB on a gray Honda with blacked-out plates, but if the killer was smart, that car would already be parked in a garage somewhere, out of view of the public. Finding where that car was stashed was their best bet now.

Charli couldn't get the way the minister had turned toward the shooter out of her mind. Was this a random shooting, or had the victim known his murderer?

And if the pair were acquaintances, what in the world had a pastor of a small inner-city church done for his killer to think he deserved such a fate?

4

Back at the precinct, Charli leaned back in her desk chair and stretched her arms above her head. Although it wasn't even near lunchtime yet, the morning's events made it seem like she'd put in a full day's work already.

The security camera footage Charli and Matthew were able to find was scarce, mostly from traffic light cameras. Matthew was sifting through the footage, starting from the cameras closest to the river where the victim had been shot. After the two closest cameras didn't show the gray Honda, the detectives had concluded the vehicle had likely turned into a residential neighborhood very soon after the riverside shooting. After that, the shooter could have gone anywhere.

Still, Matthew was continuing to make his way through the rest of their footage, just in case. It couldn't hurt to be too careful. Their next stop was at Victor Layne's home to speak to his wife. But since she'd just been informed of the death, they wanted to give her some time to begin to process her grief privately before bombarding her with questions about her husband's life.

Charli curled one leg under her while she sat on her chair

and started typing in "Cornerstone Presbyterian." The website that popped up was dated, and in place of the little arrow icon was a biblical cross.

She scanned through the home page with grainy photos of women with permed hair and dresses with shoulder pads. Charli squinted to get a better look at the pictures. The men's hairstyles seemed foreign too. She glanced at Matthew and tried to imagine her partner with slicked back hair and curtain bangs.

"What's so funny?"

Oops.

She hadn't realized she'd laughed out loud.

"Nothing. Just…reading about Victor Layne's church."

Charli dragged the cross icon to a lime green "About the Church" page. Victor Layne was listed as the minister, with a few short sentences about how he was married to his wife and spent his weekends gardening. Apparently, Pastor Layne must have served as minister for quite a while. Charli doubted that anything had been changed on the site since women were allowed to own a credit card without a man attached to the account.

Surely there was more information on the internet about Cornerstone Presbyterian. After a few more minutes of searching, she found the church's Facebook page. It wasn't even listed on the website, but it popped up in a search, and it linked to a YouTube page where recent Sunday sermons were posted.

Oddly enough, the YouTube page wasn't under the church's name. Someone by the name of Jeremy Abbott had posted the videos. Who was Jeremy Abbott? She jotted the question down.

He didn't appear to be in any of the videos of the Sunday services. Only Pastor Layne and the choir were seen standing on the platform.

During the most recent sermon, the minister spoke about how loving one's neighbor had no boundaries. He expanded on this to speak about how LGBTQ brothers and sisters were not any less deserving of God's love than the rest of humanity. Charli was pleasantly surprised at how progressive the message was.

Another thought struck Charli. If Pastor Layne had known the person who shot him—and the video footage certainly pointed in that direction—could it be a church member?

And if he was preaching progressive policy, Charli had to believe there were older conservatives in the church who didn't agree with his views.

While it could seem like a stretch that anyone would kill the pastor for his opinions, it took only one religious zealot to take such an extreme step. And people became extremely entrenched in their belief systems. Plenty of people thought their religious beliefs were worth dying—or even killing—for.

She made a note to look at the statistics of how many wars were fought for the sake of religion and was disappointed in herself for not already knowing.

Charli clicked back onto the Facebook page to skim through reviews. Perhaps there would be a nasty one that would point her in the right direction. Any intelligent killer would make sure their intentions remained unannounced on the internet, but if this murder was impulsive, they might not have thought things through.

She didn't find a single one-star review, though. A few two- and three-star reviews were there, but none of those mentioned the pastor or the ideology of the church. Most were complaints about how the building wasn't well maintained or how the church wasn't in the best neighborhood.

The five-star reviews all raved about Pastor Layne's

preaching, though. One person mentioned they were so grateful that their minister had given decades of his life to Cornerstone Presbyterian.

Ahh, so he had been there a long time.

When Charli clicked back to the home page, there was a new post. The name Jeremy Abbott once again caught Charli's eye. He had made the post only five minutes prior.

It is with deep regret and great sorrow that I announce that our beloved Pastor Victor Layne was killed in a drive-by shooting. I wish I had more information to give, but as of now, this appears to be a senseless crime. One thing I do know is that God's plan is at work at all times. I don't yet understand his reason for taking our minister from us this way, but I trust his guidance. His wife is asking for privacy at this time. Please lift her up in your prayers and check this page for updates as I learn more information.

Charli wrinkled her nose. This was the kind of mentality she didn't understand. It wasn't necessarily that Charli didn't believe in a higher power, and she wasn't averse to the idea that there was a god. She just didn't spend a lot of time thinking about the possibility because it always made Madeline come to mind.

The idea that God would allow so much torture was heinous. Why? Why would He allow one of His loyal followers to die in such a gruesome way? Why would He allow a fifteen-year-old girl to witness the event, knowing it would become a lifelong trauma?

People had told Charli similar things when she had lost her best friend.

"Everything happens for a reason."

"This will all make sense one day."

Well, it was almost a decade later, and still, nothing made sense. What a horrendous thing to tell a teenage girl. Why would Madeline have to die for some bigger plan to take place? And why couldn't those plans be made without Charli having to lose her very best friend?

Even if Charli's life had somehow turned out better for Madeline's death—which it hadn't—she'd have to be a narcissist to feel grateful for that.

Oh, Madeline lost her entire future, but at least Charli's life improved over time. That was insanity.

"You okay there, Charli?"

Charli's heart pounded in her chest, her breathing heavy. She glanced up at Matthew, who was staring right at her.

She willed her heartbeat to slow down. Ever since she'd gotten those letters from Madeline's supposed killer, she'd been on edge. She had to do something to get a grip on her emotions.

She flashed her partner what she hoped was a convincing smile. "Yeah, I'm fine." Charli considered venting to Matthew, but her emotions were bubbling up like a volcano threatening to spew lava. Vocalizing her thoughts and risking an explosion was probably not her best option right now. Besides, they had a killer to catch at the moment. "Come check out this post."

Matthew wheeled his chair over to her, his black boots scurrying against the floor. "Might as well. I just got done with all the video footage and didn't find a thing."

"Well, maybe I've got something here. I've been looking into the socials of Cornerstone Presbyterian. Turns out, Victor Layne was a very progressive minister. Just last week, he was preaching about rights for the gay community. It makes me wonder if perhaps someone violent disagreed with his belief system."

"And who is this?" Matthew nodded toward the screen as he read the post. "Who is Jeremy Abbott?"

"I'm not sure." Charli leaned forward, peering at Jeremy's profile photo.

Matthew shook his head. "Something is off about this post. It sounds almost grateful that something happened to Victor."

Although Charli understood exactly what Matthew was talking about, she wasn't so sure that it was a red flag. "I know, but this is just kinda how churchgoers speak. I've heard this sentiment shared again and again at funerals."

Matthew's mouth twinged at the edge. "That's a little disturbing, but okay. I'd still like to know who he is. Did you read the comments?"

"There weren't any when it was posted. It's only been a few minutes."

Matthew reached for Charli's mouse. "I bet there are some now. Let's refresh."

Sure enough, several people had commented on Jeremy's post.

I cannot believe this. Not our minister. I will be praying for everyone tonight. I cannot stop crying.

Oh, Jeremy. You must be devastated. Nobody worked with him more closely than you did. Where are you now? Can I bring you some dinner?

Charli hovered over that comment. "So, Jeremy worked closely with him, huh?"

Matthew stood from his chair and stretched his arms. "Maybe that means he had something to gain from his passing. I mean, I don't know how churches work, but this could potentially move him up in the hierarchy, right?"

"Really depends on his role." Another post appeared, grabbing Charli's attention. "Oh, hey, looks like he replied."

I'm at Cornerstone, and I'll be here all week for anyone who would like to visit and pray. I hope we can all provide peace for each other during this difficult time.

Matthew kicked his chair back to his desk. "I guess we know where to find him."

Charli was already grabbing her stuff. "We should go there now. It would give Pastor Layne's wife some time to herself before we have to interview her. She's next on my list. And it seems like Jeremy is the best person within the church to talk to if he's taking the lead on announcing this."

Matthew grabbed his cell phone from his desk and shoved it in his pocket. "I'm ready when you are."

5

The cold steel of my Glock gleamed as I wiped the outside with oxygen bleach. As much as I loved my gun and didn't want to corrode it, I didn't want to take the chance of having someone else's DNA on my weapon.

Maybe that wasn't necessary, but I couldn't be too careful. It was better to be safe than sorry, as my mother had always told me. I liked to be meticulous about cleaning my guns, regardless, even when I hadn't just shot someone in cold blood.

The reminder made me smile.

Yes. I...a man who'd never even set a trap for mice...had killed another human being. On purpose. With premeditation.

With glee.

The memory flooded back, like rain washing me clean of all my sins. No, it was better than being washed by the rain because this was a sin that could never be rescinded. It was final. I hadn't done something quite this final in my entire life.

Hell, even if I didn't like to keep my guns sparkling clean,

I would've sat in this room for hours wiping down this beauty just so I could relive the moment.

The years had flown by, and it had been a while since I'd felt in touch with my weapons. Like a lot of hobbies, I'd forgotten about them when I got busy with all the routine aspects of my life. I kept them on hand, of course. But when I first went to a shooting range with some friends in high school, it sparked a full-on obsession. I used to go to the range every single weekend to practice, and I even got pretty damn good at skeet shooting.

Back then, I never wanted to use my guns for anything other than target practice. It wasn't like I was born some psycho. I didn't grow up torturing little animals or anything. This was nothing like that.

No, before this, I'd been a normal, happy person. My entire future had been before me, and I had hopes and dreams just like anyone. Sure, I had my struggles, but who didn't? Maybe there had been times when I felt like my wife didn't understand me at all, or maybe I thought I deserved to be making a bit more money. I'd always accepted these flaws in my life as normal.

Until now.

Now, no one could relate to what I was currently going through. And it pissed me off when they said they could. Or worse, when they said they could make it better.

I called bullshit. And my bullets of this morning punctuated that statement.

Bam. Bam. Bam.

No more empty promises coming from the good pastor's mouth. Why had it taken me so long to realize I could stop that type of madness?

As satisfying as the morning had been, I couldn't stop myself from being pissed that it had taken me so long to stand up for myself.

All my life, I had tried to be moral. I'd followed the path laid out in front of me dutifully. No matter how much I fought with my wife, I stayed a loyal husband. Even when I got paid shit, I showed up for work on time every day.

And this was what I got for it?

Hell no.

I wasn't gonna accept that. It took one horrible event to realize I'd been living my life as a total pussy. All those years, I had done what everyone wanted of me.

Not anymore.

Now, I was going to be a man, a real man. Men took things into their own hands. They didn't stand by and let the world walk all over them. And they didn't let their bitch of a wife nag them half to death.

When I looked back on my life, even my obsession with guns seemed so weak. It used to make me feel like a man to go to a shooting range and hit a fake target with the outline of a person on it. Why? I was shooting a damn piece of paper. What was manly about that?

Nothing.

It had all been a farce. Technology had given us these devices that held the power to end a life. There was no greater power, and I'd been wasting it on skeet shooting. What a fool I'd been.

But now, I saw the world in a new light. These guns that I once used as a weakling could be my deliverance. Using them to right every wrong in my life would restore the power that I'd mistakenly given away to so many others.

After I'd cleaned my gun for what seemed like hours, I was satisfied that I had polished every last millimeter. But I wasn't exactly eager to put it down and go into the living room. How I hated that living room. My wife had decorated it with frilly white curtains, a couch cover dotted with lilac flowers, and a faux rabbit rug.

Yeah...really.

The fake rabbit fur was really the icing on the cake of my loser life. A real man would've gone out there and killed a rabbit to make a rug. My wife bought the damn thing on Etsy, and it wasn't even real. Even worse, she *liked* it that way.

I could just hear her now. *"Why would I want an innocent animal killed so I can decorate my house? That seems so cruel."*

Coming from a woman who ate some part of an animal at every meal, I could only shake my head.

Until recently, I hadn't noticed that she, too, was powerless. It was hard to even remember why we'd come together in the first place. What did I like about her? Had I ever liked her? Or had I just felt obligated to get married and settle down because that was expected of me?

But none of that mattered now. What was done was done, although it didn't mean I had to sit my ass in that girly living room. Not anymore.

I reached for my shotgun, wanting to clean it next. With the small movement, a wave of nausea hit me. "No..." Nearly overwhelmed by the sensation, I reached out and rested a hand on the crude worktable, willing the feeling to go away. It didn't. At least not for many, many minutes.

When the nausea finally started to subside, I took my time with my shotgun. That would give me more time to sit in the garage, the only space I now felt comfortable in within my house.

The garage wasn't decorated, not even a little bit. The concrete was cracked along the walls, the shelves unpainted and stained with years of use. But I had a simple chair out here and my gun shelf, and it was the only place in the house my wife hadn't completely ruined with her garish tastes.

As if on cue, the garage door opened.

Think of the devil and she appears.

Sometimes, I swore she could sense when I was thinking negatively about her. Since I was as far away from the door of the house as I possibly could be, I doubted she heard me sigh under my breath. Not that it mattered. Not anymore.

"Dinner is ready." Her high-pitched voice was like nails on a chalkboard, and the nausea threatened to return, as if stirred by her words.

I didn't even look up. I didn't want her to see the level of loathing I had for her in my eyes. "What is it?"

Even without glancing her way, I could picture her in a pair of her too tight sweats or one of her frumpy dresses sticking to all those curves. Not the good, womanly kind of curves I used to like so much.

"White bean soup."

Seriously?

Soup for dinner. Who the hell had soup for dinner? That wasn't even food. It was like having a drink for a meal. I didn't care about her damn liquid meal. I'd rather pull out a TV dinner, so I chose not to answer.

"Are you coming?" Her squeaky, *isn't life grand* voice failed to hide her annoyance.

I finally glanced up at her and regretted it immediately. Unwashed hair pulled into a messy bun. That was about the only way she wore it these days. Sweats too tight on a frame that had been steadily growing bigger over the years. The lines in her forehead had grown deep from her permanent scowl.

She looked nothing like the day I married her.

She didn't act like it either, which was the bigger issue.

"No. I'm busy." My voice was flat, even though I wanted to scream each syllable in her direction.

"Are you serious? Cleaning your guns is busy?" Her nasally voice became louder, reverberating off the garage walls. "Can't that wait?"

Was she kidding me? Couldn't she see that I was going through my own personal hell?

What the hell is wrong with her? With a jerk of my wrist, I snapped my shotgun closed, the sound reverberating throughout the large room.

The bitch jumped back a step, causing the fat in her cheeks to bounce. "P-please don't do that. It freaks me out."

When I didn't bother answering, she let out a huff and turned to leave. My pulse quickened, and I pointed my shotgun at her back.

It would be so easy. I knew that now. In a split second, I could put her out of her misery.

Put her out of *my* misery.

Power coursed through my veins as I became something primal, an animal on the hunt. I could do it. I really could.

"There's no time like the present. Do it now."

It was so tempting to listen to that little voice that had been growing louder inside of me each and every day, but the timing wasn't right just yet.

I patted the place where the voice I'd named Damian lived. "Later."

Even though the word was barely more than a whisper, my hag of a wife turned on her heel. Taken by surprise, I lowered the barrel before she could see what I'd done, my heart beating hard.

"I'd really like it if you'd have dinner with me." Deep frown lines formed on the edges of her cheeks.

Much to my chagrin, it was probably best I kept her on my good side. Who knew when I'd need her to vouch for me?

"Yeah, I'll be there in a minute." I kept my face unmoving, unsmiling. If I had to give in to her, I refused to show any fake happiness about the deed.

The little smirk that lifted her cheeks as I conceded to her caused bile to rise up my throat. I swallowed it down.

Once again, I had to remind myself of my goals. I could put up with this woman while I executed my plan. There was no other choice.

I knew I could be caught before fulfilling my mission. After all, I was no expert. Someone was going to find me out. It was probably a miracle I hadn't been caught already. All I did was put some electrical tape on my license plate and turn down a one-way street two blocks down from the river.

After I had shot the repugnant Victor Layne, I thought the police would be knocking on my door right away. But cops just weren't that quick, apparently, which worked out in my favor.

All I needed was a little more time.

And a little less money.

Smiling at my clever turn of phrase, I tucked my hands into my pockets as I strode to the door. The smooth metal touching my fingers was soothing.

One down.

Five remaining.

Jingling my change, I faced my wife in the kitchen as she filled a bowl with her vile soup with a victorious smile. Little did she know that her time on this planet was nearly at an end.

And she wasn't the only one.

6

Charli could see what the two- and three-star reviews were talking about. There was chipped plaster on the corners of the walls, and with every step she took, the wooden floorboards creaked. But although Cornerstone Presbyterian was a bit on the dingy side, she smiled at how the worn pews were shiny from years of devoted church members sitting on them. The building certainly had character.

The fact that so many people praised this church had to be a testimony to Pastor Layne's talents as a minister. Obviously, people were willing to forego a high-end place to worship in exchange for listening to sermons with substance.

Charli glanced around the main room, but it was empty. Where was Jeremy Abbott?

Focusing on finding the man instead of her surroundings, Charli avoided looking directly at the altar. One of the last times Charli had been in a church was for Madeline's funeral. When she'd entered the building, she hadn't expected the memory to be so triggering. But even though

Cornerstone Presbyterian wasn't the location of the funeral, it had a similar vibe. She supposed all churches did.

Charli could practically hear the choir singing songs of mourning, her friend's ashes in an urn at the front of the room next to a series of photos. After Madeline's time spent in a marshy shallow grave, her body couldn't even be displayed in a casket.

Matthew put a hand on Charli's shoulder. "You all good? You're looking a little red in the face."

Only a little? Then why did her skin feel like it was burning off her bones?

"I'm fine. It's just a little warm in here."

Doubt flickered in Matthew's eyes, but he'd just have to wait if he wanted her to share more. Jeremy Abbott could come into the room at any moment, and Charli didn't want to be sharing such a personal story when he did. She was here to do her job.

"You think so? It feels great to me. I think the air conditioner is on." Matthew reached up in the direction of one of the ceiling vents.

"I'm surprised they're able to keep it running with the state of things." Charli stepped in front of him, stretching up to feel for herself. Being so much shorter than Matthew, she could barely catch the draft from the high ceilings.

Charli flinched when a voice behind her spoke up. "In Savannah, you've got to keep the air-conditioning a priority in the budget, right?"

The voice wasn't accusing but teasing. Charli and Matthew turned to find Jeremy Abbott standing before them. At least, Charli was pretty sure it was Jeremy. He fit the profile picture she'd seen to a T. If Charli had to guess, she'd say the man was in his late twenties.

His dirty blond hair was parted on the right side and combed over, the longer hair on top of his head tousled with some sort of gel. As he strode closer to them, his black dress shoes clicked against the creaking floorboards, his button-down sky blue shirt tucked into pressed black slacks.

"Allow me to introduce myself. I'm Jeremy Abbott, the assistant to Pastor Layne." The warm smile on his face fell as the last words left his lips. "Well, I guess I was."

Charli took a step forward. "That's why we're here, actually. I'm very sorry for the loss of your minister. I'm Detective Cross. This is my partner, Detective Church. We're investigating the shooting of Victor Layne."

Jeremy's eyes widened, enhancing their moss green hue. "Oh, how grateful I am to meet you." He moved toward them both, putting two hands around Charli's right one before she got a chance to stop him.

She did her best not to recoil from the touch. "We're glad to hear that because we're hoping you can help us learn more about your minister's life."

"I'd love to. Please, come have a seat." As Jeremy turned around, he pulled his shoulders back. There was something about how straight he stood. Most people had a little more slouch in their step.

Jeremy led them both to a pew. Charli had no desire to sit in a church pew, but refusing might put him on edge, and it was important to keep him relaxed for any questioning. She sat down in a worn spot in the wood, trying not to cringe as she wondered how many people had sat there before.

Butt to butt. Swell.

"What can I help you with?" Jeremy folded his hands in his lap, consistent with his rigid posture.

Charli pulled out her notebook and a black ink pen. "When did you last speak to Pastor Layne?"

"I believe it was last Sunday. Sometimes we speak... spoke...during the week about church business, but not always." The smile that was left on Abbott's face from their introduction had faded. His gaze drifted off to the side.

Matthew shifted in his seat, as though trying to make the wood more comfortable. "What kind of work did you do with Pastor Layne?"

"Oh, a little bit of everything, really. I'm his right-hand man. I film the services, run the church's social media pages, set up for Sunday service, keep the building tidy, come in for special church events, answer calls. It would be easier to say what I don't do." There was a hint of pride in his tone, and he gave a wistful smile.

Matthew nodded, but Charli noted the gears turning in his head. "Do you plan to take over for him as minister?"

The question was so innocent out of Matthew's mouth that Jeremy didn't bat an eye. But Charli knew her partner was trying to establish a possible motive.

Jeremy Abbott sighed, relaxing his posture just a bit. "Unfortunately, that won't be possible. I'm still in the middle of my seminary studies. We had discussed me one day becoming a minister, but that's still a couple years off. I'm just trying my best to be at the church to field calls and pray with our church members. And I'm sure I'll help the new minister out extensively, whoever they may be."

This didn't seem like the kind of thing Jeremy Abbott could lie about and get away with it. Unless he was harboring some secret hatred toward the deceased minister, there wasn't an obvious motive for him to involve himself in the death of Victor Layne.

Charli glanced up from her notebook. "Have you ever seen any of the churchgoers express animosity toward Pastor Layne?"

Jeremy's lips tightened, and his gaze drifted once again. "Hmm. I really can't think of anything. Pastor Layne was loved by our congregation, and he had such a calm, peaceful demeanor. It's hard to imagine anyone getting frustrated with him, let alone spiteful." He jerked his head up, knitting his brows as he spoke. "Wait! We did get an odd email several months ago."

Now they were getting somewhere. "What do you mean by odd?"

Jeremy met Charli's gaze. "It wasn't overly aggressive, but it did seem angry. Someone was upset that the minister had been discussing that transgender 'Bathroom Bill' in church."

Charli jotted down a note. "When I was skimming through some of the minister's recent sermons online, I noticed he spoke on LGBTQ rights. Is that common for him?"

Jeremy drew in a deep breath. "This is confidential information that, normally, I would not share with anyone. And, frankly, I'm not even sure I'm right about this. But Pastor Layne's passion for the gay community started only a few months ago. He had always been very open to all people, don't get me wrong, but he hadn't preached about this specifically until recently."

Excitement swelled inside Charli. "What changed?"

Glancing toward the door, Jeremy lowered his voice. "I suspect that a member of our youth group may have confided their sexuality or gender identity to him, and he wanted to make this individual feel included."

Charli's brow furrowed. "But you're not sure about that?"

"Well, he never mentioned it to me, but there have been rumors about one of the children. And all the teens in our church are very tight-knit. They often confide in the pastor or me. So, it's partially a hunch, but one I believe in very strongly." He gave a short little nod, causing his tousled hair to bounce just a bit.

Though Charli had a complicated personal history with religion, she admired Pastor Layne for having been such a positive force for the youth of his church. Charli's religious father had insisted his wife and daughter attend church when she was growing up. She would never have confided in one of her church elders. They'd always talked down to her, anyway. And if she ever dared to say anything that questioned their teachings, she'd been chastised.

For Pastor Layne to craft sermons just to make a young person feel accepted was honorable, and it was a shame that such a good-hearted person had been taken from the world too soon. Giving herself a mental shake, Charli did her best to put aside the warm feelings this triggered within her and stay as detached from the minister as possible. As upsetting as it was that he had been wrenched from his community, letting her emotions run rampant would only deter her focus.

Charli wouldn't let that happen. "You have no idea who the sender of that email was?"

Jeremy shook his head. "No, it was anonymous. I'd be happy to give you access to the email address it was found on. Hopefully, it's still in the inbox. I don't delete anything, but it's possible Pastor Layne might have."

"Yes, we're definitely going to have our tech guys take a look at it. Thank you." The cyber guys were good at their jobs, including recovering IP addresses from sent emails. Perhaps this would be the lead Charli needed.

Although one angry email didn't exactly mean that person had killed Pastor Layne, it was the only motive they'd found at the moment.

Unless, maybe, there was another one Jeremy could come up with. "Is there anything else you think we should know about Pastor Layne or the congregation? Any other suspicious activities?"

Jeremy's head bobbed from side to side. "No, the pastor was the opposite of suspicious. That man was an open book.

And I just…" His voice cracked and he lifted a fist to his mouth. "Excuse me. I'm sorry. I just can't fathom why someone would do this to Pastor Layne. Honestly, Detectives, I believe this murder has to be random."

Matthew gave Jeremy a curious glance. "What makes you say that?"

"Because anyone who knew Pastor Layne would never want to kill him. He was a saint." Abbott let out a long sigh, pausing before he spoke again. "I don't just say that because he's a minister either. I have met many other ministers, and plenty of them are snakes. But not Pastor Layne. I chose to work as his assistant specifically while doing my studies because he is a fantastic man, and I'm sure our entire congregation would agree with me. He volunteered at local homeless shelters when he wasn't at the church. And every morning, he delivered sandwiches to the homeless on his bicycle. He even helped build houses for Habitat for Humanity. Victor Layne was invested in his community."

Charli smoothed a stray fringe of hair behind her ear. "Did Pastor Layne keep his schedule on a computer? And do you know which homeless people he fed?"

Jeremy shrugged. "I don't think he used the computer for scheduling, but he did have an appointment book he used for all his church activities and volunteer work. He was such a caring person."

Genuine admiration shone in Abbott's eyes, and a pang hit Charli's heart at the thought of this man no longer having his mentor. "Do you have access to that book?"

The assistant shook his head. "He usually kept it on his desk here at the church, but he often took it home with him. The book isn't on his desk today. Perhaps you could check with Mrs. Layne."

"We'll do that. We're deeply sorry for your loss, Mr. Abbott. Thank you for your assistance." Charli pulled her card out of her pocket. "We'll leave you to your work, but please call us if anything comes to mind."

Jeremy took the card and tucked it into his pocket. "I will. Thank you so much."

There wasn't much to thank the detectives for quite yet. But after learning about the good work Victor Layne had done for his community, Charli was more resolved than ever to nail his murderer.

7

M atthew used his left arm to shut the passenger door to Charli's car. Although his right arm was fully functional again, he still had a bit of residual pain from a stab wound he'd gotten during an encounter with a criminal not too long ago.

Not that he could complain. He was alive and well while a man who many compared to a saint was lying in the morgue.

Life sure wasn't fair.

Shaking his pity party off, Matthew refocused on the case. His hunch about Jeremy Abbott's Facebook post being suspicious faded after their meeting with him. Charli had been right.

Again.

Just like she'd said, all that weird, cheerful chatter on his Facebook post was just the words of a religious man trying to make sense of a heinous crime.

Now it was back to the drawing board. Before they left, they'd gotten the login information for Pastor Layne's email account. They'd already called the information into the cyber security team before making their way out to the pastor's house where they hoped his wife would be.

But man, Matthew wasn't looking forward to it. Interviewing widows was by far one of his least favorite job duties. The woman had found out only hours ago that her husband had passed. No, not just that he had passed, but that his death had been a senseless murder.

Matthew had never lost anyone in such a horrible way. His experiences with death had all been by sickness or random accident. Not that those deaths hadn't stung. When he lost his beloved grandma to cancer, he'd been destroyed. But knowing that it was the circle of life, he was able to eventually move on from her death. He missed his grandma, but he didn't feel haunted by her passing. She'd lived a full, happy life.

That was in stark contrast to what Charli had gone through with Madeline, whose passing had seemed to change her as a person. Even ten years later, she was fixated on her best friend's death. Granted, she was now getting letters from Madeline's supposed killer. That was enough to make anyone crazy. But the problem was, she'd been stuck on Madeline even before the letters.

Of course, it all made sense to Matthew. Someone dying of an accident or disease was part of the process of life and was something one learned to accept.

But when someone murdered a loved one? That wasn't natural. It wasn't normal. Something like that was never supposed to happen. When an individual decided to end another human's life on purpose, the event was agonizing for friends and family.

And to have that murderer still running loose…?

Which reminded him…he had another murderer to catch right now. And another loved one to question.

Matthew let out a long sigh. He dreaded the interview he

would soon have with Pastor Layne's wife. To get his mind off it, he struck up a conversation of a very different type.

"I tried that ticking thing, you know."

"Ticking what?" Judging from the puzzled expression on Charli's face, she must have been lost in her own thoughts. She shook her head as if to clear it. "Do you mean TikTok?"

Shit.

Yeah. That sounded more correct. He hated being this old and out of touch.

"Right. Anyway, I sent Chelsea a TikTok video instead of trying to text with her."

Charli grinned for the first time that day. "How did it go?"

"Pretty well, actually." Matthew smiled at the memory of the interaction with his daughter. Maybe it wasn't conventional, but he would take whatever he could get. "She didn't answer with words. But I sent her a video of this cat throwing a toy into the air and then chasing it, like it was playing fetch with itself. And she sent me a video back of another cat crying at a mountain lion outside."

Though Charli couldn't look at Matthew while driving, her apple cheeks protruded with a smile. "That's so great, Matt. See, now you're really speaking teenager."

"Can't say I understand the language yet." Matthew fiddled with his seat belt as it dug into his shoulder, but that wasn't nearly as uncomfortable as trying to make chitchat with a teen. "Took me a week to figure out that suss meant suspicious and something that's good is bussin'."

"No cap?"

He pointed a finger at her. "Don't you start!"

Her grin grew wider. "Well, old man, it takes years to become fluent in a language, and teenager is one of the harder ones to learn." Charli gave him a quick little wink as she teased him. "But you're getting there."

He snorted. "Getting there like a turtle whose head is

stuck inside its shell, maybe, but you're right. At least Chelsea's answering my messages again. Sometimes, anyway."

He was desperate for real conversation, but it was a start.

Charli pulled up in front of a modest, white house not far from the Wilmington River and squinted at the faded number on the porch. "I think we're here."

The neighborhood was a little questionable but not the worst in Savannah. Old cars lined the street. Many houses had a chain-link fence rather than white picket.

But the house in front of them was one of the best maintained homes on the block. The grass was trimmed, and the front lawn was lined with rose bushes. There was no chipping paint, though it appeared to be the norm on their street.

Whatever beauty the exterior of the house had was marred by the sound coming from inside, though. The second Matthew's foot hit the porch, a horrendous wail echoed from the open front window. He could hazard a guess it came from the pastor's wife.

"This is going to suck." Matthew kept his voice low, though he doubted very much he could be heard over the wailing.

Charli grimaced and shrugged. "It needs to be done, though." She reached up and rang the doorbell.

She wasn't wrong. Although Matthew would rather let Victor's widow grieve in peace, they needed to get her story today while it was still fresh in her mind. The longer they waited, the more the details of this day would blur together.

Charli had reminded him many times that this was a well-studied phenomenon. Witness testimonies became more clouded with each day that passed. Not that the widow was a witness, but she was one of the last people to see her husband. They needed to know how he acted before leaving or if anything strange had happened in his life recently.

They waited a moment for someone to answer the door, but when it swung open, Matthew was surprised to find the blonde woman who answered appeared dry-eyed. Although she sported a frown, her face showed no sign of grief.

"Can I help you?" There was a twang of annoyance in the question. The woman wiped her hands on a billowing blue kitchen apron, a cloud of flour rising from the fabric.

"Hello. I'm Detective Church, and this is my partner, Detective Cross. Are you Mrs. Layne?"

"No. That would be my sister. My name's Anne Kingston." Her lips fell into a deeper frown, causing previously unnoticeable lines to form on her cheeks. "Does this really need to happen now? She can barely form a coherent sentence."

"I'm afraid so." Charli stepped forward, so she was closer to the door than Matthew was.

The widow's sister didn't even attempt to muffle a groan before she gestured for them to enter. "Okay, come in. She's in the living room to your right. I need to get back to cooking. We've had a horde of church members bringing food and visiting, but she says she only wants my pot pie. It's her favorite."

"Is anyone with her now?"

Anne pressed her lips together. "I sent everyone away to let her rest." She gave them a pointed look.

Charli raised a placating hand. "We'll be as quick as we can. I promise."

The woman snorted and led them down a short hallway. As blunt as she was with the detectives, her gentleness with her sister was in stark contrast. "Lydia, honey, some detectives are here to talk to you about Victor." She leaned down to Mrs. Layne, who was curled up in a fetal position on the couch.

The scene left an ache in Matthew's stomach. Wrapped in

a blue and white quilt on the sofa, Mrs. Layne didn't look up right away. Her tears were quieter now, but they were still streaming down her cheeks. Though she had to be in her sixties, she gave Matthew the impression of a helpless infant with her legs curled under herself. Grief was a funny thing.

"Hello, Detectives." Mrs. Layne's voice was hoarse as she swiped a hand across her cheeks. With effort, she forced herself into a seated position.

Charli smiled softly at the grief-stricken woman, compassion shining in her eyes. "Hello, Mrs. Layne. I'm Detective Cross, and this is my partner, Detective Church. We'd like to offer our condolences for the loss of your husband. I know this isn't the best time to speak to us, but we're hoping you could answer a few questions about your husband and shed some light on anyone who might have wanted to harm him."

Mrs. Layne nodded and mopped her face with a handful of tissues that had seen better days. "Anything to help you catch who did this to my Victor."

The living room was set up so two floral couches sat on either side of a glass coffee table. The look was classic, with an old hutch displaying vintage china on the far-right wall of the room. Although no television was in sight, rows of oak shelves lined the opposite wall, filled with countless colorful volumes. Charli and Matthew sat on the matching floral couch on the opposite side of Mrs. Layne.

The widow's grief was palpable, and Matthew couldn't help but wonder if anyone would ever grieve him this way. His ex-wife sure wouldn't, but even Chelsea wasn't speaking to him, unless TikTok videos counted. Would anyone care this much about him if he was shot in the streets?

Matthew swallowed the lump in his throat. "We wanted to ask you about the last time you spoke with your husband."

Weak gasps came from Mrs. Layne as tears continued to stream down her face. "Just before he left for his bike ride. I don't work. I haven't since the day I met Victor. I...I was baking a pound cake when he left. I think it...burned."

The cadence of her words was stunted, stopping and starting at unusual times. Mrs. Layne was nearly catatonic.

Charli fidgeted with the short strands of her hair. She took in a deep breath, then spoke in a soothing tone. "Mrs. Layne, do you know of anyone who had any kind of conflict with your husband?"

Mrs. Layne glanced at Charli, clutching at the throw wrapped around her. "Victor didn't fight with anybody. He couldn't have fought with a fly. My husband was so sweet. In all our years of marriage, he never raised his voice to me. Not even once."

One thing that was consistent was everyone's description of Victor. But being in this line of work, Matthew was well aware being kind didn't protect a person from murder. "What about someone who disagreed with his actions within the church? Can you think of anyone like that?"

"No." The word was a whisper.

Matthew hated to ask this next question because of her fragile state, but it had to be done. "And did anyone else see you here at home, Mrs. Layne?"

Grief alone was not enough of an alibi. The detectives had to make sure they could rule out Victor's wife as a suspect.

While a lot of loved ones often expressed anger at this question, knowing it implied they played a part in the crime, she didn't bat an eye. Matthew was willing to bet she was as kindhearted as everyone said her husband had been.

"My sister was here. We visit every week." Her hand slid across the edge of her blanket, back and forth. It wasn't unusual for the detectives to see repetitive movement from grieving loved ones. This was common for someone trying to comfort themselves. "And...we have one of those fancy security cameras, if you need more proof."

Charli's head lifted. "Why do you have a security camera?"

Mrs. Layne's nostrils flared, and it was the first emotion besides sadness that Matthew had seen from the woman. "Victor bought it for me for Christmas one year. He wanted to make sure I was safe at home when he wasn't here with me." Another sob escaped Mrs. Layne as she buried her face in her hands.

Matthew cleared his throat. "Did your husband keep any kind of appointment book, Mrs. Layne?"

The woman raised her head, her brow furrowed. "I... think so. I don't think it's here, though."

If the book wasn't at the church and it wasn't here, where was it? It had to be here at his house somewhere. Perhaps Mrs. Layne would remember its whereabouts later when she was thinking more clearly.

Matthew wasn't sure how many answers they were going to get from her before she completely shut down, so he prioritized the rest of his questions. "Do you know anyone with a gray or silver Honda?"

Mrs. Layne pulled the blanket even tighter around her body. "I don't think so, but...I don't know. So many people attend our church. There are so many cars in the parking lot every Sunday, and many others ride the bus or walk."

Matthew didn't know if there would still be a church service this upcoming Sunday in light of Victor's death. But whenever the next service was, the detectives would be there to scour the lot. Only an idiot would drive the same car to that church, but not every perp was smart. And sometimes, they got arrogant or sloppy.

Since Mrs. Layne hadn't been present at the scene of the crime, there weren't many identifying details she could provide. But Charli and Matthew continued to question her about Victor's life. Matthew held onto the possibility that a red flag might pop up to help them in their investigation.

But the more questions they asked, the more Mrs. Layne shut down until, eventually, she stopped answering altogether. That was when her sister popped back into the room.

"She needs rest. You two can come back another time, yes?" The woman was no longer wearing an apron, and Matthew took a deep breath as the aroma of chicken and garlic filled the home.

Charli popped to her feet. "Yes, of course. We'll head out so you two can eat." She placed her card on the coffee table. "But, please, call us if anything else comes to mind. If we have any further questions, we'll be in touch."

On the way out, Charli asked Mrs. Layne's sister where she was at the time of the crime, which confirmed the alibi, and she showed the detectives the video from the doorbell camera. She'd come over with a tray of cookies for them to enjoy over tea. That explained why Mrs. Layne was baking a cake, since she wasn't great at explaining that herself.

As soon as they shut the door behind them, Matthew glanced over at Charli to find her eyes were nearly as hollow as Mrs. Layne's.

"Everything okay?" Matthew was a broken record today with that question. But every time Charli had answered that she was fine, she seemed anything but.

"Yeah. It just never gets easier, does it? Seeing people like that is rough." Charli ran a hand through her short locks, pushing the hair off her forehead.

"No, it doesn't." But Matthew knew there was more to it than that. "But are you all right? Something feels off."

Charli finally relented. "I can't get the letters about Madeline out of my head. Since the first one arrived, I'm constantly wondering if her killer is actually out there, keeping an eye on me."

Matthew worried the same. He didn't say this to Charli— she likely wouldn't take it well—but he drove by her house sometimes while running errands just to check on her. "There is always that chance the letters were mafia related."

Not long ago, he and Charli had caught a local funeral home cremating bodies for the mafia. The boss didn't much like his favorite disposal system being shut down, putting him and Charli on their radars. And maybe their hitlist.

Charli strode down the driveway toward her car. "Don't remind me. Being threatened by the mafia is just another fun element to this mess. But I think it's too early to say that the letters have stopped. Every day now, I open my mailbox with gloved hands like a lunatic."

Matthew pulled open the passenger side door. "You aren't a lunatic, Charli. You're a detective. A damn good one."

"Maybe it's possible to be both lunatic and detective. I think you need to be a little crazy to work this job."

She had a point.

8

Charli was stuck in a waiting game back at the precinct. Before she and Matthew could move forward, they needed to hear back from both forensics and ballistics. Although a list of anyone who owned a gray or silver Honda sedan had already been compiled, it was one hell of a list. No way would Charli and Matthew be able to meet with every registered owner. Even after cutting out all the cars made in the last eight years, since the vehicle in question was likely older, the list was exhaustive.

But it was still a useful tool. They'd be able to cross-reference it with registered owners of the gun model used, narrowing the list down. And if the gun was rare, they might finally have a solid lead. But they wouldn't be able to narrow down that list until they knew the model of the gun.

Too much they still didn't know.

Charli didn't like it.

As she pored over her interview notes from the meetings with Mrs. Layne and Mr. Abbott, her mind wandered to Madeline. Again.

Knowing it would continue to wander there until she

paused just long enough to acknowledge the intrusion, Charli sighed. She would let her mind go there for two minutes max, she bargained with herself before opening her desk drawer and pulling out photocopies of the letters she'd received in the middle of their last case.

Keeping these copies at work was more than a little obsessive, and she was aware of that. What was worse? She had more copies at home. This wasn't healthy. If Charli had a therapist, they'd probably recommend she didn't stare at these letters on a daily basis.

But Charli didn't care if it was healthy. Between the sinister notes and being followed by the mafia, she was a little rattled these days.

She peered at the first letter, willing her hands not to tremble like they had the first time she'd read it.

Ten years and you still haven't found me. Do you give up?

As it did each time she read the words, a chill ran down her spine. Charli closed her eyes and pinched the bridge of her nose, but it did nothing to relieve the pounding in her temples.

She held up the second note, the one that had been in her mailbox at home rather than at the precinct.

And to think...if we'd gotten you that day, along with your friend, you wouldn't be worrying about all of this. What a heavy burden it must be.

Charli shoved the letters back in the desk, resisting the urge to slam the drawer. Who the hell had sent them? Was someone in the mafia—or any individual or group she'd pissed off during her stint with the Charleston PD—impersonating Madeline's killer just to scare the living daylights out of her?

Or were the letters from the murderer himself? And was there one killer or two? She wasn't sure about anything anymore.

Although she'd been rummaging through old files from when her friend had been abducted, the letters didn't make anything click. They didn't add any relevant information to Madeline's case, and they didn't give Charli a clue as to who the killer was.

As much as she wanted to believe the messages were just another mafia scare tactic, the possibility that they could be from Madeline's murderer ate at her day and night. What if he had been watching Charli for the past ten years, waiting to strike again? And what if Madeline had only been the start of a vicious killing spree, and he'd tortured and murdered countless victims over the years? The thought made Charli sick to her stomach.

What could she do, though? She'd exhausted every avenue.

A ringing phone jolted her out of her musings, and she swiveled her chair around to face Matthew's desk.

"Detective Church here." Frowning, Matthew scribbled a few notes down. "Okay, great. Thanks for the update."

Charli was on the edge of her seat. "Who was it?"

"Ballistics. They were able to identify the gun." Matthew tucked his phone back into the pocket of his black blazer.

This should have been good news, but there wasn't even a hint of excitement on Matthew's face. Charli leaned forward, her hands on her knees. "And?"

Matthew tossed his head back before giving it an exaggerated shake. "And it's a Glock 19."

Well, that made sense, but the knowledge only deflated Charli more. They'd been hoping for an unpopular gun that could help them narrow down their list of suspects.

Probably the most common handgun in the country, it seemed that every new gun owner went out and bought a Glock 19. On the one hand, this was good news. They could compare the gray and silver Honda list to anyone who owned that specific weapon in Savannah.

But this was the South. Since everyone and their mother had a gun, this wasn't going to make their list as small as they'd hoped.

Matthew rolled his chair closer to his desk and pulled up the National Tracing Center. "Well, we're sure in for a long night."

"You're telling me." Charli leaned back into her chair. Earlier, she had told herself that playing the waiting game was the worst part of her job. Well, she was wrong. It was cross-referencing lists.

Matthew scrolled the cursor down on his computer screen. "I can enlist Janice's help to get us through a chunk of this."

Charli scrubbed her hands over her face. "Ah, great. Looks like my night is about to get even longer."

Matthew stopped mid-scroll, cocking one eyebrow at Charli. "Seriously?"

Charli returned his stare. "If you think she can quit gawking over you long enough to really help, go ahead."

Pink climbed its way up her partner's cheeks, and Charli turned back to her computer to hide her grin.

Did Matthew think getting Detective Janice Piper to help would somehow make everything go more smoothly? Faster, maybe, but only if Janice could stop making eye babies with Matt long enough for them to get the job done. At least the flirting was one-sided.

Since Matthew's divorce, the woman was practically all over him. Well, her actions may be subtle, but to Charli, her ploy was obvious. Besides, the woman loathed her. Janice's glares of disdain at Charli turned into gushing smiles in a hot minute whenever Matthew entered the room.

The astute detective she was, Charli was aware of her subtle actions and simply didn't want her friend and partner to get caught in Janine's manipulations. Not because Charli had any romantic interest in Matthew herself. She thought of him as a big brother and friend, and she would fight to the death for him.

Especially man-eating viper snakes like Janine.

Like the desperate golden retriever she was, Janice popped her head in only seconds after Matthew made the call. Maybe golden retriever wasn't the best description of her. The woman had ears like a basset hound. Even from a few feet down the hall, had she heard them speaking about her?

"Did you call for me, Matthew?" The sugary sweet tone was like nails on a chalkboard.

Charli shuddered. *Gag me now.*

How the hell did Matthew not see that Janice was desperate to date him...and more? They sometimes went out for drinks after work, but he swore to Charli it was just as friends and showed no interest in her advances. That woman wasn't capable of doing anything as just friends with Matthew, and it was obvious to Charli that she wanted much more.

Now that Charli thought about it, Matthew hadn't gotten drinks with Janice in quite some time. Maybe her partner was savvier about the detective's not-so-subtle flirting than he let on. She made a mental note to quiz him about it later.

"Yeah, we could use some extra manpower if you're available this evening. We have to cross-reference a list of gray or silver Honda sedans with people who own a Glock 19." Matthew flashed her his usual polite smile.

As soon as the slender redhead pranced through the door, she angled herself away from Charli, as far as she could turn while still facing Matthew. He didn't even seem to notice. *Surprise, surprise.* Men could be so clueless about these things.

Janice batted her mascara-laden eyes and toyed with the top button of her silky black shirt.

"Sure! I can help you out with that." If her grin got any wider, her face was liable to split in half. She gave a dainty toss of her head as she flipped her hair over her shoulder.

Of course, she could help Matthew out with that. It was never, "I can help you guys" or "I can help you and Charli."

"Thanks, Janice!" Charli pasted the most genuine smile she could muster on her face. "It'll make this night go by a lot faster."

Janice didn't even turn to Charli. "Just shoot me an email with the names to look up." With another bat of her lashes, she flitted out the door with a little too much pep in her step.

Admittedly, any name that Charli didn't have to look up herself was a win. She settled into her chair, readying herself to camp out in her office for the rest of the evening.

9

Light had just begun to stream through Charli's window, telling her that a complete sunrise hadn't happened just yet. Charli could avoid the light on her face every morning if she moved her bed to another wall, but she'd placed it in this spot on purpose to keep herself from oversleeping.

This morning, she could use the extra rest, though. She, Matthew, and Janice had been at the precinct late the night before doing background checks on their cross-referenced list. They came across a few people with criminal records but no violent or gun offenses. Most were petty theft or possession.

Their list was far too long to start calling people to ask about their whereabouts the day Victor Layne died, but Charli had emailed Jeremy Abbott asking for a list of congregation members anyway. Maybe, if this was church related, comparing that list to their current one would single somebody out.

If they could find anyone on their list who actually knew Pastor Layne, it would be a great breakthrough in their investigation. The email went out late the night before, so Charli was hoping when she rolled over to grab her phone off her nightstand, she'd have an answer waiting for her.

Her vision still blurry from sleep, Charli scrolled through her phone. It was 7:01, and there was no email response yet. There was, however, a call from the sergeant.

Damn. How did I miss that?

The missed call was only a few minutes ago, but she knew Sergeant Ruth Morris hated when a phone call went to voicemail. Charli dialed back right away.

She didn't even get a chance to speak before Ruth started barking orders. "I need you at the bus stop next to the Trail-head Coffee Shop. Another shooting took place fifteen minutes ago."

Surely, she hadn't heard that right.

Chilled to her core and immediately on hyper alert, Charli put the phone on speaker so she could wrestle into some clothes as she was briefed.

"A shooting similar to the one we've already got?"

"Almost exactly the same. A gray car was spotted. It was a quick drive-by. This appears to be our perp. Two shootings in two days. This is turning into a nightmare." Ruth's voice was infused with worry, a stark contrast to her typical determined, no-nonsense tone.

"We'll get over there right away."

"You better. Because news vans are going to show up any moment. They're going to be all over this double drive-by. I want my best detectives at the scene ten minutes ago."

"I'm on it." Charli tossed her phone on the bed as she tugged on her shoes.

Moments later, she ran a comb through her pixie cut, which was just enough to keep her from being disheveled. Not much time had passed between their last case, but she'd managed to squeeze in some time for a much needed trim and was grateful the strands went into position easily enough. She didn't need to look like a peacock on television.

As she settled into her car, she called her partner, letting him know she was on her way. The Trailhead Coffee Shop was not far from Matthew's apartment, so they were there quick. But not quick enough. As Ruth predicted, there was already a news van on the corner of the street, just beyond the caution tape that had been placed around the bus stop and coffee shop.

Walking into this scene was a déjà vu moment for Charli. A throng of onlookers had gathered around the caution tape as several beat cops held them back. Someone had covered the victim with a sheet. As the detectives approached, Officer Anderson was yet again on the scene as the first responding officer.

Charli flashed a small smile as she signed herself into the logbook, Matthew following after her. "Good morning, again. If you wanted to see us this bad, you could just stop by the precinct."

A ghost of a smile tugged at the corners of the officer's lips. "For real. This is getting old."

Charli retrieved her notebook and pen from her pocket. "So, what do you know?"

"Our victim is an African American x-ray technician in her late thirties, Gretta Franklin. She was dressed in navy scrubs. Her identification card for work was clipped to her shirt, which was how we were able to identify her so quickly. We've got one witness, a cashier at the coffee shop, who confirms a gray sedan." He waved over his shoulder to the building. "There were multiple shots. Forensics still needs to identify the location of those bullets and whether they all hit Ms. Franklin."

Charli jotted down a note. "Has the next of kin been informed?"

"Not yet." Officer Anderson rubbed his eyes. "It looks like the victim wasn't married. She owns her own condo, but nobody is on the title with her. No emergency contacts listed in her phone."

Matthew stared at the puddle of blood before him. "Try calling the hospital where she works. They'll surely have some emergency information for her."

"Was about to do that next. If you guys want to head into the coffee shop to speak with our witness, an officer is inside with her. She's a sweet kid, Kayla Renfield, eighteen years old. Poor thing is shaking like a leaf."

Dammit, yet another teenager as a witness. With Madeline swirling around Charli's mind, she did not want to have to question another teen girl. But this wasn't about Charli or Madeline. She had to remind herself of that.

Kayla had a foil blanket wrapped around her shoulders as she sat at a trendy wooden coffee table at the front of the shop. She probably hoped that warming up would stave off the shivers, but Charli knew it wouldn't. If someone was shaking from fear, warmth didn't always help, but there was no point in telling her that.

The beat cop rose from the table, motioning for Charli and Matthew to have a seat in his place. They did exactly that, and Kayla eyed them wordlessly as Charli introduced them both.

"I know this feels like a terrible time for us to be asking you questions, Kayla, but we'll be as quick as we can. What did you see and hear today?"

Charli kept the question vague on purpose, allowing the witness to fill in details without any influence from the detectives.

"I didn't see it, really. I mostly heard it." Kayla fidgeted with the collar of her shirt. "I mean, I know the front of the store is all glass, but I had my back turned to it because I was blending a frappé for a call-in order. Usually, when I blend, I can't hear a thing. Customers will yell at me from a few feet away, and I won't even flinch. But this...I heard it so clear. It was so loud."

"Were there any customers present?" Charli doubted this since they would've been held for questioning too, but she needed to clarify.

Kayla rubbed her fingers back and forth along the band of a baby blue smartwatch on the opposite wrist. "No, it was just me and two to-go orders."

"And what did you hear, exactly?" Matthew leaned back onto the cushioned blue booth seat, putting his hands on his lap.

"I'd just turned off the mixer when I heard three really loud bangs. Some of the frappé spilled onto the floor because I turned around so fast, but I still didn't know what had happened." Kayla's eyes filled with tears, and she quickly swiped them away. "I saw a car drive by. At first, I didn't see the woman, but then..."

Charli hated to push her, but she had no choice. "What did you do then?"

"I called 9-1-1. There was so much blood." Kayla bit her lip, her eyes closing for a moment as she recounted the events. "I ran outside, but the operator told me not to move her. No matter how loud I screamed, she didn't react. The operator wanted me to see if she had a pulse, but there was so much blood. I'm so stupid. At first, I didn't even realize she was gone forever."

It bothered Charli deeply to witness yet another young woman harbor so much guilt for a crime that was out of her control. "That's very understandable, Kayla. When something this traumatic happens, it can be difficult for what you're seeing to register. It was very brave of you to try to help her."

The young woman's eyes filled with tears again. "There was nothing I could do."

Charli smiled softly. "And that's not your fault. Remember that in the days and weeks to come, okay?"

Kayla swiped at her cheeks, her head making a juddering up and down motion. "I'll try."

It was the most Charli could ask for in the moment. Wanting to refocus the young woman's brain with a question, Charli asked, "What do you remember about that car?"

Kayla seemed to give herself a mental shake, blinking hard and lifting her chin. "All I know is it was gray. It looked old, like the kind of car you see in a junkyard. But I don't know a lot about cars."

Matthew moved his hands from his lap, putting them on the table as he leaned in. "Could you see a license plate? Or any words on the back of the car?"

Kayla pulled her blanket around herself a little tighter. "No. I didn't even really see the back. It turned the corner so fast."

"That's okay. I'm sure it happened quickly." Charli glanced up at the ceiling of the coffee shop to find a small security camera. "Do you know if that camera works?"

Kayla drew in a deep breath. "Yes, but I don't get to see it. All the camera feeds go into an app on my boss's phone. My boss should be here any moment now. He can help you with that."

That was a relief. "That's perfect, Kayla. I'm sure that's going to be very helpful with our case. Are there any other details you can remember regarding what happened?"

Once again, tears welled in Kayla's eyes as they met Charli's. "No. And what I remember, I just want to forget."

Charli's heart shattered for her. She knew from personal experience that the teenager was never going to forget the events she'd just witnessed. This day was probably burned into her memory forever, just as the day of Madeline's disappearance was burned into Charli's.

But unlike Charli, Kayla wouldn't have to worry for the rest of her life that the killer was still roaming the streets because Charli was going to find this sociopath. She wouldn't give up until she did.

10

B ack at the station, Matthew waited for the footage from the coffee shop to load. While he willed the upload to complete, a ding on his phone grabbed his attention.

His immediate hope was that he'd flip his shiny silver phone over to find that Chelsea had sent him another TikTok video or maybe even a text message. Although he and his daughter mainly conversed through videos and memes, at least they were communicating on some level. That was an improvement from not too long ago when Matthew couldn't even get her to answer him. Not that she answered him every time now, but progress was progress.

Their relationship was still tense, to say the least. But the tips Charli had given Matthew about sending funny videos had helped immensely. Admittedly, there was still a shadow of loneliness cloaking him like a wet blanket. Sending videos was better than nothing, but it wasn't a conversation. He still didn't know how his daughter spent her days. How did she like school? What was her favorite subject? Had she made some new friends? Was she dating someone?

She'd better not be.

Matthew shuddered at the thought, but his daughter was a teenager. The time for her to take an interest in boys had come, whether he liked it or not. But Matthew always thought when his daughter did begin dating, he'd be there to answer the door while wearing his badge and his gun. A little intimidation from Chelsea's detective father would've kept the boys in line.

When Matthew grabbed his phone, he found it wasn't Chelsea who'd messaged him, but Rebecca Larson, the shrink friend that Charli was trying to connect him with.

Hi, Matthew. So glad you reached out. Charli said you might.

Matthew let out a breath in a slow, steady stream. He hadn't even realized he'd been holding it. Before he'd left for work this morning, he'd sent a text to Rebecca, introducing himself and telling her he'd like to chat about his daughter.

Charli had been trying to talk him into speaking with her child counselor friend about Chelsea for a while now, and he'd finally gained the courage to do so. The idea of talking to a stranger about his issues with his daughter just felt so… weird. Where did he even start?

Before he had a chance to respond, his phone lit up.

So, tell me a little bit about your daughter.

Okay, he could do that. His relationship with Chelsea may be on thin ice right now, but there was one thing he was certain of. She was an amazing kid.

Well, Chelsea recently turned fifteen. She's smart, funny, and beautiful, but I'm pretty sure most dads think that about their daughters. Oh, and she plays the violin, although I haven't heard her play yet.

He smiled softly. Although he'd been hesitant to speak about his issues with his daughter to a stranger, just talking about her felt good. If nothing else, it was a step in the right direction.

He glanced down at Rebecca's reply.

Violin, huh? That's impressive. How often do you get to see her?

A dull ache throbbed in Matthew's chest. Since the divorce, he'd barely seen Chelsea at all.

Not often, unfortunately, which is part of the problem. And for the longest time since her mom and I divorced, she wouldn't speak to me. Now at least she answers my texts. Well, some of the time.

Three dots appeared on Matthew's phone, and soon after, another message popped up.

That's a tough age. Tough for parents too. Don't get discouraged when she doesn't text back. Teenagers have a lot of distractions these days. Have you tried sending her memes or funny videos?

Matthew grinned, and he glanced at his partner, who was absorbed in something at her desk.

Funny you should say that. Charli suggested the same thing not too long ago, and it really seems to help. I usually get an emoji out of her, at least. But half the time, when I try to ask her about her day or how she's doing, she doesn't respond. And she's the queen of one-word answers.

He leaned back in his chair and stretched his arms out in front of him, clasping his hands together. His phone dinged. Boy, was Rebecca fast.

Hmm...at least you get some sort of response when you send her funny memes and videos. Maybe it's a good idea to keep the conversation light as much as you can. When you're with your daughter, what do the two of you like to do?

If Matthew could spend time with his daughter, he didn't care what they did. Hell, he would watch paint dry with Chelsea if it meant they could be in the same room together.

Honestly, I don't know what she likes to do anymore. She always had fun when I took her shopping. And we both like to watch movies.

Before Matthew had time to think about other activities they enjoyed doing together, Rebecca was typing her reply.

Have you ever tried watching a movie together long-distance?

You can put the same movie on and FaceTime while you watch it. Or you could just text each other while you watch. If you chat about the movie and keep it light, maybe she would open up a little. Plus, you'd be spending time together.

Why hadn't he thought of that himself?

What a great idea. Thanks! I'm going to suggest that to her as soon as my schedule allows.

Much like Charli, Rebecca was easy to talk to, and her concern for Matthew and Chelsea seemed genuine. If her texts were any indication, Matthew had a feeling the woman was incredible at her job.

His screen lit up again.

You're welcome! You know, Halloween is just around the corner. You could mail her a package with candy and popcorn and plan a scary movie date.

"Who keeps texting you?" Charli swiveled around in her chair. With all the time they spent together, she knew he wasn't the kind of guy to get regular texts. She probably thought it was related to the case.

Matthew typed out a quick *gotta go, will text again later* reply before tucking his phone into the pocket of his black slacks.

"Rebecca."

Charli's entire face lit with interest. "Really? So, you finally decided to take my advice?"

Matthew rolled his eyes. "Sure did. And you know what? I'm glad you twisted my arm. She's already had some great ideas about how to connect more with Chelsea."

Charli flashed him a grin. "That's awesome, Matt. Rebecca is wonderful, and I'm so happy that you're talking to her."

"So am I. It's a relief to know that I'm taking a step in the right direction."

Matthew glanced at his computer. Consumed by his

phone, he hadn't even noticed that the security footage had uploaded.

Matthew scrolled through the footage until he found the time stamp he was looking for. The street had been quiet at that time. It was a bit too early for most people to be traveling to work, so that was no surprise.

The forest green bus stop bench on the sidewalk right outside the coffee shop was well lit from a streetlight on the corner. On the other side of the street was an empty field with development signs. At some point, a shop or two was supposed to be built there, but the developers hadn't broken ground yet.

To Matthew's chagrin, none of the other businesses, including a photography studio and a real estate office, were open at the time of the drive-by. That meant no witnesses, but officers would soon be going business to business to determine if any additional security cameras might exist.

On the bright side, at least there were fewer people to be traumatized by the tragedy that had occurred outside early that morning, but what Matthew wouldn't have given for a witness who had seen the shooter.

"If wishes were horses and all that bull…"

He focused on the video as Gretta approached the bus stop and took a seat, setting her purse on the bench next to her. That purse was still being examined by forensics for any DNA evidence.

A few cars passed by. Thankfully, this camera feed was a lot clearer than their last, so Matthew could tell that none of the cars were the gray Honda they were looking for. Then, bam, a beat-up Honda straight out of the early 2000s crept in front of the bus stop.

Matthew paused the footage. "Charli, I've got the gray Honda on scene now if you want to come take a look."

The wheels on Charli's chair rattled over the bumpy tile

of their office floor. She used the heel of her boot to stop herself once she reached Matthew's desk, where he resumed the video playback.

Even with Matthew slowing down the footage, the scene unfolded quickly. While the gray Honda had stopped next to Victor Layne for a total of fourteen seconds, this time, the vehicle was only in front of Gretta for less than three seconds before the driver unloaded a couple of shots into her body. One bullet ripped through the plexiglass overhang that surrounded the bus stop bench.

The bastard even shot Gretta a little salute before driving off.

Unbelievable.

Rewinding the video, Matthew focused on the driver this time. The camera angle gave the detectives a perfect view of the culprit. Not that it did much good. The shooter was wearing a black hoodie over a ski mask. Every facial feature except his eyes were a blur. And even with the higher definition of this video feed, there wasn't quite enough clarity to identify an eye color.

Matthew smacked his hand against the desk. "And, of course, he's not visible."

Charli scooted her chair closer to Matthew's. "Can you see what color is on his license plate?"

Matthew peered at the paused footage. "Must be a dark blue or a black. Maybe electrical tape? It's got a sheen to it. Have you heard back from Jeremy Abbott?"

Charli shook her head. "Maybe he's not up yet. Probably had a late night with the news of the minister's death."

"Well, once we get that, maybe we can narrow down our list of Honda or Glock 19 owners."

Charli leaned back in her chair, folding her arms across her chest. Even sitting down, she was so short that Matthew had to look down on her. "Let's hope so. Because right now, we don't have much information to go off of."

A knock at the door grabbed their attention. Ruth stood there with narrowed eyes and a tensed jawline. Matthew could always tell when she was close to exploding because her jaw would move back and forth ever so slightly while she ground her teeth together.

Her lips were set in a thin line. "My office now, please."

11

C harli was well aware that when their sergeant got like this, she wasn't upset with them. She was irritated at the situation.

Ruth shut her office door behind her and strode toward her desk. "Are you two any closer to getting me a solid lead?"

Charli plopped down next to Matthew in one of the chairs in front of Ruth's desk. "Nothing sticks out between our lists of Glock 19 owners and gray Honda owners, but they're both hefty lists. I'm still waiting to hear back from the minister's assistant for a list of churchgoers."

Ruth didn't sit down. Instead, she paced back and forth behind her desk, her cropped black curls glimmering under the LED lights.

"No more waiting." Ruth's voice was cold as ice. "If you don't have that list by the time you leave my office, you need to go back to the church immediately. Not only do we need to know if we can get a match on these three lists, but I want to know if Gretta Franklin attended that church."

Matthew leaned forward and propped his left elbow on

the desk, resting his chin in his palm. "You think there's a link between Gretta and the minister?"

Ruth continued to pace back and forth. "While I hope there's a link, I actually don't know shit. Have you two happened to check any of the local news stations?"

Was Ruth kidding? Charli barely had time for a bathroom break. "Not yet, though I'm assuming they're reporting on these two shootings."

"They're comparing this to the Beltway sniper attacks." A wrinkle formed on Ruth's forehead as she let out a long sigh.

Though Ruth's face was serious, Charli couldn't stop a bark of laughter from escaping her mouth. She wiped the incredulous look off her face when Ruth's head snapped toward hers, daggers in her eyes.

Ruth held her gaze until she finally spoke. "Is this a joke to you, Detective?"

Charli clenched her hands in her lap. "Of course not. That wasn't a humorous laugh at all. It just pisses me off how the media try to cause hysteria in communities."

Sergeant Morris's eyes softened the tiniest bit. "Peace isn't profitable, Detective. Hysteria is. Pain is. Fear is. And if the media can serve all those emotions up on a pretty little platter to the public, they'll do it."

True that.

Steering the conversation back on track, Charli nodded. "It's a little early for those hysterics, though, and we can't let ourselves get caught up in them. The Beltway snipers killed ten people, injuring several others. It was a pair of men who were highly coordinated. We have no reason to think this is more than just one guy. And I don't mean to diminish the deaths of these individuals, but we're talking about two victims."

Ruth's face hardened, and Charli's pulse quickened. "Two victims in two days, Detective Cross. Need I remind you that the Beltway attacks took place over three weeks? If our killer keeps up with this speed, he'll outdo the two of them in no time at all. And we really have no reason to suspect this is one person because, so far, we know next to nothing." Her voice rose on that last word, and she squeezed her eyes shut, a vein in her temple protruding.

Matthew chanced a glance at Ruth, whose eyes were still closed, before leaning in to whisper to Charli. "Don't mess with her murder face."

Charli rolled her eyes so hard they hurt. "Sergeant," Ruth's eyes flew open, and Charli took a deep breath, "we know how the media sensationalizes crime, but we're not going to lose ten people. This could be a number of things, maybe some gang initiation crap gone wrong. I don't think we're looking at a highly organized criminal proceeding. The person has tape on their license plate for crying out loud."

Ruth stalked toward Charli, stopping about a foot in front of her chair. "I think you sound extremely confident for someone who can't even give me one possible suspect. Two killings in twenty-four hours, Detective Cross. Our suspect is organized enough to keep you from immediately identifying him. Instead of focusing on what the media is doing, maybe you should find out who attends the minister's church. Find me a link between Gretta and the minister, and then I'll be more inclined to agree with you."

But wasn't Ruth the one focusing on the media? Sure, what the media put out as public information made her job harder, but the sergeant was the one who had brought up the media in the first place.

Charli opened her mouth to speak, but Matthew beat her to it. "If we can't get a hold of Abbott, we'll go to the church right away. And if Gretta Franklin does attend the church, we'll know this isn't random." Her partner had a knack for stepping into a conversation if things began to get intense.

But why was Ruth jumping to the worst possible conclusion before they even knew whether the shootings were connected? Yes, the shooter had worn a mask and covered up their license plate, but that was the bare minimum in terms of hiding their identity. If the shooter attended the same church or was in any way connected with the victims, they would find out pretty quick. Charli hoped that was the case.

Even if it wasn't, it was still outlandish to compare this to the Beltway snipers. With Matthew keeping the peace, Charli had no desire to restart her argument with Ruth. Their stress levels were high and would stay that way until they had a suspect.

Resisting the urge to share her thoughts further, Charli pulled out her phone to check her email. Her most recent response was, indeed, from Jeremy Abbott.

Charli nearly sagged with relief. "We've got the list. We can go make our comparisons right away. Hopefully, that will give us some much needed answers."

The lines in Ruth's face softened, but the urgency still rang out in her voice. "Is Gretta Franklin on the list?"

Charli opened the document. With the finder tool, she searched Gretta's name.

Nothing.

Charli searched every variation of misspelling on Gretta that she could think of. Greta, Grets, Greeta, and then did the same for Franklin.

Still nothing.

"Not according to his list."

Ruth walked around to the back of her desk and sank into her chair. "Get me that link, you two. Find out how these drive-bys are connected. And I need it done yesterday."

Charli nearly tripped over Matthew's foot as she scurried out of her chair. "We're on it."

12

When I pulled up to the diner, my heart was pounding so hard that I could actually feel my pulse in my ears. The sensation should be disconcerting, even inducing panic.

But it wasn't.

As adrenaline shot through my system, it calmed every nerve.

Never before would I have believed that choosing each victim, stalking them, and ridding this world of one more piece of human scum would bring me such a deep sense of satisfaction.

What had that old bastard harped on? Peace? Joy? There was no peace or joy in this miserable life. And he could shove his peace and joy up his stiff ass. Oh, wait. He couldn't. He was dead.

Hollow laughter rang out, and I jumped, startled to my very core.

Whirling to check that no one had slipped into my back seat, I practically shouted, "Who's there?"

That same hollow laugh came again, and realization hit

me. It was only my new friend.

"Dammit, Damian," I pressed my hand to the place in which he lived, "don't scare me like that."

In response, Damian sent a searing sensation shooting through my abdomen. The pain was constant now, often accompanied by nausea. I couldn't eat, couldn't sleep, couldn't even shit without surges of pain.

Peace? Hardly.

Joy? Hell no.

Maybe I didn't have peace and joy like that always-smiling, prosperity-preaching nutjob had rambled about, but I had something much, much better.

Control.

I had ultimate control over the destiny of those who had gloated in spite of my prognosis. They'd had the nerve to tell me everything would be okay. That they would do everything in their power to make the rest of my life more comfortable. That everyone had to go some time, and we never knew when that day would come.

I had seen the pity in their eyes. Heard their empty, meaningless words. Well, I had news for them. It was time for those assholes to experience the terror and despair I lived through daily.

Every night, I woke in a pool of cold sweat, pain racking my body, fear so palpable, I could almost reach out and touch it. Only, when I woke up, the nightmare wasn't over.

But that was okay. I had come to terms with my destiny. Damian had helped me. As his whispers had grown into shouts of encouragement, I knew that, before I took my last breath on this Earth, I was going to make those bastards pay for their part in my living hell. Call it revenge. Call it karma. Whatever the hell it was, I was going to rid the world of those meaningless pieces of shit, one bullet at a time.

Memories from the past assailed me. I'd spent my life

trying so hard to be good. I'd aimed to be a truly moral person at the cost of everything else because, in my heart, I actually was convinced that being a decent person would bring me the life I desired.

Years ago, I'd settled for marrying a simple-minded woman because she liked me, and I liked…no, tolerated, her, and I thought we could make a life together. Where had that gotten me? Chained to a nagging, whining heifer who hadn't even noticed how distressed I'd been. A wife who, had she truly taken care of me, would've seen the signs before I did.

Sitting in the living room, watching her do those damn cat puzzles, I never once felt the thrill I now did sitting parked outside this diner. I'd wasted too many years.

"Not anymore."

"You're right, Damian. Not anymore."

My gaze was glued to the neon glow of the "open" sign outside the diner because, any moment now, a man was going to step out of those double doors and walk toward his car. A man who didn't deserve to be breathing.

Glancing around, I began to worry that this might not be the best place and time. The other shootings had been in the early morning where darkness had helped cover my tracks. Maybe I should wait and—

Pain shot through my gut, twisting around to bite into my lower back. I squeezed my eyes shut, pressing my lips together to hold in a scream.

"Do it now!"

As Damian continued his torturous assault on my body, I knew he was right. I couldn't wait, no matter the cost.

"O-okay…"

The grip of pain released, leaving me sweating and breathless in the driver's seat. As I peeled my fingers from the steering wheel, I cursed myself. I should have known better than to question Damian's timing.

He was right to remind me of just how little time I had left. I couldn't waste it. There was still so much left to do.

And if I was caught? I shook my head, forcing the thought away.

I'd been careful.

I'd spent weeks following my victims, learning their patterns and schedules. That's how I knew to be outside of this diner right then. Human beings were predictable creatures.

Pulling my cap farther down on my forehead, and pulling the mask up to cover my mouth and nose, I wasn't worried about being noticed. In this old beat-up car, I was just about as forgettable as a person could be.

When I was finished with my killing spree, though, the entire nation would know my name.

People said that a person had to find a passion in life. That it was impossible to reach true happiness until someone had something they did day in and day out that made them happy. Well, I supposed this was it for me.

I drew in a shuddering breath. If only I'd known this earlier. Better late than never.

With a sigh, I pulled out my binoculars. Maybe I would spot him through a window.

Bingo.

He was seated in a booth on the right side of the building flirting with the staff.

How pathetic.

As the bastard chatted with the pretty server, I traded my binoculars for a handgun stashed in my glovebox. Reaching into my pocket, I pulled out one of its contents.

Now I was ready.

It was almost showtime.

13

R oger Stanton ran his fingers along the outside of the diner menu, but he didn't open it.

"Your usual again, Roger?" Lacy's red curls bobbed as she walked, falling just above the large bosom that always seemed to be popping out of her baby blue uniform.

Roger didn't have to glance down at the menu, and Lacy knew that.

He grinned at the server, winking before she walked away. "You know it, Lacy. Thanks so much. You're a real doll."

Though no doll he'd ever seen had those perfect hips that formed her hourglass shape, dimples in the corners of her cheeks, and her signature ruby red lipstick. She could have been straight out of a 1960s magazine, which was in keeping with the diner's décor.

Roger loved coming to this place because it brought him back to a simpler time in his childhood. Years ago, his dad used to take him to an old diner with sixties décor, not unlike this place. As he closed his eyes, his mind drifted to those red leather seats and shiny metal tables where he'd sit as he slurped up a chocolate shake in an icy cold glass.

With a smile on his face, he opened his eyes, and his gaze landed on Lacy's retreating form.

If Roger was being honest with himself, he didn't come here just for the nostalgia. It certainly didn't hurt that his usual waitress was so easy on the eyes. He couldn't help but wonder if she left the top button of her blouse open on purpose for extra tips. But if she did, it certainly worked on him.

A ding from his phone had him reaching for his pocket. His dick pulsed as he read the message notification from the dating app.

I'm still looking forward to tonight. Are you?

Roger hadn't met Linda yet, but her profile photos were darling. The woman had wavy brown hair, a heart-shaped face, and eyes so blue he could swim in them. And her bio made it extremely clear that she wasn't interested in anything but a hook-up, which was exactly what he had in mind.

In his youth, he'd had to pick up women at the bar. But now, with online dating so prevalent, finding other almost fifty-somethings interested in hooking up was a piece of cake. When the first profile that caught his eye popped up, he'd swiped right, and luckily, he and Linda were all set for their little...tryst.

All in all, it was shaping up to be a pretty good day. Roger was about to eat a pastrami on rye, his favorite lunch. He had a hot date for later, and none of his employees at the mini-mart had called in today. Though after lunch, he did have to swing by to give the two employees currently working their consecutive lunch breaks. After they were both back on the clock, he'd be relaxing before dinner.

Less than ten minutes later, Lacy set a shiny red plate on

the table, loaded with steaming pastrami on rye. She patted him on the shoulder and bent over a little as she set down his soda. "Anything else I can get you, honey?"

Roger's pulse quickened as he got a glimpse of what was underneath the sassy waitress's baby blue v-neck. "I don't need anything else, Lacy. Thank you."

That wasn't altogether true, though. Roger desperately needed to see those sweet hips swing as Lacy stepped past him. Watching her sexy young body prance around in that tight little number would only benefit Roger later tonight.

Not that he ever needed much help with the ladies. At least, he didn't need help when it came to hooking up with them. Settling down with them was an entirely different story and not something he was very likely to do.

To this day, Roger didn't understand the appeal of marriage. Why the hell would he want to spend the rest of his life chained to the same woman? It wasn't realistic. He could barely do a weekend vacation with the same female.

He'd gone through his life under the assumption that he simply wasn't built like some other people were. Perhaps monogamy was a thing someone was born with. And Roger wasn't.

Didn't bother him, though. In his thirties, friends used to tell him that he was going to regret his decision. That one day, he'd be a lonely old man. He'd want a family.

No, thank you.

As Roger had witnessed his buddies get married and have kids, all he could ever think was how obnoxious it must be to wake up at two a.m. and change a diaper. As the years went by, he'd ask his friends to come out for a drink, and their wives or girlfriends would rather they stay home.

What kind of prison was that?

He much preferred the life he'd built for himself. Stanton's Mini-Mart was pretty much a cash cow, and he was able to spend every cent it produced solely on himself. He met up with women whenever the desire suited him. Overall, he had a decent life. He had no complaints.

Roger picked up the pastrami sandwich and dug in.

Mmm.

He groaned as the flavors danced on his tongue. The only issue with his favorite meal was that it could be a bit messy, and a glob of mustard fell onto his chest. He grabbed a napkin to wipe it off, but it wasn't going to stop the stain from setting in.

No worries. He had enough money to not worry about the shirt. He'd just toss it out when he got home.

As he savored the rest of his sandwich, Roger found himself glued to the little TV hanging above the cash register. He couldn't hear the news anchors talking, but he could easily read their closed-captioned words.

"Authorities have still not released the name of the second drive-by shooting victim pending the notification of next of kin, but we have it on good authority that the victim was an African American female. A witness has confirmed that a gray Honda was in the vicinity of the..."

Roger snorted under his breath. Drive-by shooters were all pussies, especially the ones who only came out when it was dark outside. He'd just have to be sure to get Linda in his bedroom before the sun set.

He could do that.

Taking a sip of tea to wash down his last bite of sandwich, Roger didn't wait for Lacy to come back around. He didn't need a check. He left cash for his meal, including a hefty tip for the sweet little server before making his way out into the parking lot to get back to the mini-mart.

But when he pushed his hand against the glass front door, something made him pause. For a brief moment—a little blip —some weird red flag went off in his brain.

There was a number of cars in the parking lot, as this particular lot shared space with several other businesses. Were any of them gray Hondas?

As his gaze swept the lot, he lost count of the vehicles that color, though many ranged from light silver to gunmetal. Could one of them belong to the shooter?

"Don't be ridiculous."

Pissed at himself for even pausing, Roger continued to push open the door. Outside, sunlight doused his skin, but he shivered in spite of the warmth.

Get a grip, man.

In his hyper-vigilant state, he fixated on a gray Honda Accord turning the corner. Sure he was about to shit his pants at the sight of the vehicle's emblem, he almost turned to run back into the diner when something about the vehicle caught his attention.

Did he know that car? The dented bumper and scrape of blue paint on the right headlight. Yes, he did.

Relief nearly turned his bones to water as he laughed at himself. Throwing up a hand in a friendly hello, he was still smiling when the vehicle pulled up beside him.

"Man, you're gonna have to park that ride." Leaning down to see the driver's face, he didn't even notice the gun peeking through the window until the barrel lifted a few inches.

"I will…soon."

Before Roger could even process what was happening, a bolt of lightning ripped through his chest. Reeling backward, he tried to catch himself when a second slug of pain took his legs out from under him, and he found himself staring up at the clear blue sky.

Something small caught the light before bouncing off his face. Another streak of lightning? An angel? The fiery gates of hell?

He wasn't sure.

As molten lava spread through his veins and hot wax boiled in his chest, Roger was only certain of one single truth...he was dying.

As his vision dimmed, a question whispered through his mind. Would anyone miss him when he was gone? Would anyone care?

He had no wife, no kids, no family.

Linda...

Even she would curse him when he stood her up.

14

Despite failing to find Gretta Franklin on the Cornerstone Presbyterian congregation list, Charli wouldn't be comfortable ruling her out as a church member until she read each name herself.

But seven hundred of them? Charli hadn't been expecting such a large following for what appeared to be a fairly small church.

A half hour later, Charli had to grudgingly agree with the sorting software. Gretta wasn't on that list no matter how badly she wanted the woman's name to appear.

"Okay, then. Let's see how many of the Cornerstone crew own a Honda."

This search took much longer, and the results were equally disappointing. While two people were revealed to be Honda owners, their cars were made within the last five years. The video footage made it clear that the car they were on the hunt for was a hell of a lot older. In addition to the dents and dings, the edges of the car were more square than rounded, a popular look in the nineties. Cars today typically weren't boxy like that.

Even more surprising, none of the names came up on the list of owners of a Glock 19, which Charli found odd, considering how conservative religious folk sometimes were. Surely, some of the people who attended that church had to be gun owners. But none of those guns were a Glock 19. None that were registered anyway.

Charli let out an audible groan as she pushed her short hair off her forehead.

Matthew clicked his tongue from behind her. "I take it you haven't found anything."

Charli rolled her eyes. "Excellent deduction skills, Sherlock."

"Hardy har." Matthew clicked his mouse, sliding it over the black pad next to his keyboard. "In fact, Sherlock has nothing on me."

Hope stirred in Charli's chest. She'd been riding along a trail only to come up with dead ends, and she desperately needed Matthew to find something she hadn't. "What are you searching for?"

"I'm doing a deeper dive on Gretta's social media accounts." Matthew tapped his computer screen. "She didn't seem like a very active user, and she barely had any friends, but I'm wondering if her profile might have interacted with the church or a church member at some point. She may not be on their list of attendees, but that doesn't mean she didn't attend one random Sunday or something."

Charli rose from her chair, the wheels squeaking against the tile, to walk around Matthew's desk. "Find anything yet?"

He glanced at her over his shoulder, a wide grin on his face. "Hold your horses, partner. This will take a while." He heaved a big sigh as he turned to face her. "A few years ago, there's a tweet where she talks about being agnostic. If that's still true, I'm thinking we might not have a link."

Damn.

With shoulders slumped, Charli headed back to her chair and plopped down. Not only was this going to continue to stress out their sergeant, but it meant their jobs as investigators had just gotten even more difficult. Random murders were usually more complicated to investigate.

But just because the church didn't appear to be a link between Gretta and the minister, that didn't mean there wasn't one.

"Matt, we really need to get Gretta's patient list from the hospital. What chance do you think we have on getting that warrant?"

After interviewing Gretta's boss and many of her coworkers earlier that morning, they'd applied for a warrant to have access to Gretta's patient list for the past three months.

Matthew leaned back in his chair, linking his hands behind his head. "What chance do you think that Ruth will get off our backs?" He raised his voice a few octaves. "I want this case solved yesterday!"

Charli's eyes widened, and she wilted in her chair. *Smooth, Matt. Real smooth. Your timing really sucks.*

Matthew threw up his hands. "What?"

With an almost imperceptible nod, Charli cleared her throat, a tentative grin tugging at her lips.

"Wait, don't tell me she's standing right behind me." Matthew's voice was just above a whisper.

"Yes, Detective Church, I'm standing right behind you. And you really need to work on your impersonation skills."

Matthew spun around. "Sergeant, I—"

"Save it, Detective." Ruth jammed her hands on her hips. "And get Janice to follow up on that warrant. I need you both."

Hope deflating like a stray balloon running into a tree branch, Charli just stared at her sergeant, praying she wasn't reading what she thought she was reading on the other woman's face. "You're kidding."

Not even a whole day had passed. Two shootings today?

Ruth placed a finger on her temple, rubbing it in slow circles before inclining her head in a single nod. "And from what I've overheard of your conversation, I assume you've got no link for me between Gretta Franklin and Victor Layne?"

Charli swallowed hard. "Not yet."

Though Charli had argued with her boss about it, she now had a gnawing sensation in her stomach when she thought of the Beltway snipers.

What was going to happen if there was no link? What if these killings were completely random, and they continued? As Ruth had pointed out, the Beltway killings happened over the span of several weeks.

If these shootings continued at this pace for that long, they'd have a body count way higher than the Beltway snipers. Although Charli liked to think that she was a top-notch detective, the FBI had one hell of a team on the Beltway case, and that had been a hard nut to crack. Without a connection between the victims, who knew how long it would be before they had a suspect?

Charli wasn't going to spiral, though. Although the last thing they wanted was another shooting on the same day, she had to view this as another opportunity to find evidence.

She took a deep breath before facing Ruth with a newfound determination. "So, where are we headed?"

15

A crowd gathered outside of the yellow caution tape lining the crime scene, and Charli had to sidestep to avoid smacking into a lookie-loo who wasn't watching where he was going.

Since Ruth had briefed the detectives as she walked with them to Charli's car, they didn't spend much time with Officer Anderson, who was yet again present at the scene. According to Ruth, their victim—Roger Stanton—was identified by the ID in his wallet. He was a single man who owned a local mini-mart just a few blocks from where they now stood. Matthew had searched for his name on the church members' list using his phone, and it didn't pop up.

This crowd was considerably bigger than the ones at the other shootings because this one had taken place in the middle of the day. It had also taken place in a small shopping center that boasted a specialty craft shop, a shoe store, and the diner where the murder took place.

As Charli glanced around, she noted that the parking lot wasn't completely full, and officers were currently stopping people from entering or leaving. Still, everyone who was here was now waiting to learn what had happened.

Instead of being pissed, Charli hoped this meant there were more witnesses for her and Matthew to speak to.

As Charli made her way through the crowd, she spotted the medical examiner standing just outside a screen that had been erected to preserve the victim's dignity. With the interest in the drive-by shootings growing, Charli was glad the crime scene had ordered the precaution.

She wasn't surprised that he was already here. Dr. Randal Soames didn't always come out to a crime scene, as much of the forensic work was done back at his lab. But three shootings in two days? That was certainly enough to get him out into the field...fast. After signing the logbook and donning gloves, the detectives made their way over to the privacy screen.

Inside, they found Dr. Soames waiting patiently for the forensic photographer to finish his duties. Slumped over a concrete parking lot bumper, the victim appeared to be in his late forties or early fifties. His crystal blue eyes hung open, staring out into space. But they weren't really staring, were they? Those eyes no longer functioned at all.

Who did you last see?

There had been a time in her career when Charli wished there was some way to retrieve the last few seconds from a victim's brain. That she could pull it out and rewind the last moments of his life.

This was one of those times.

"Not a pretty sight, huh?"

Startled by Soames's question, Charli forced herself away from wishful thinking and back to the here and now.

Examining the victim more fully, she started at his hair and ran her gaze downward. Flecks of blood dotted the man's cheeks, but that was where normalcy stopped. Below his neck was nothing but a gory mess. Flesh, blood, and bone had exploded out of his back into the parking space next to him.

Charli cleared her throat. "Hollow point?"

Soames nodded. "Based on the expansion of the exit wound, that's very likely." Squatting beside the victim, he peered closer at the wounds. "Interesting that the shooter decided to focus his shots on the torso this time. Whoever our killer is, I believe they're a good shot."

Charli thought she knew where he was going with that but asked anyway. "What do you mean?"

"Because, at the first two scenes, we found only one stray bullet that didn't first penetrate the victims, and that was with Ms. Franklin. One of the bullets went through the plexiglass at the bus stop." Soames turned around and gestured toward their most recent victim. "We suspect this was at close range. The decision to shoot somewhere besides the head would appear intentional."

Soames was right, now that he mentioned it. Charli glanced at her partner, who had turned a sickly shade of green. He always struggled with these gory scenes far more than Charli did.

Not that Charli wasn't bothered, of course. The victims she saw always shook her, though potentially in a different way than they did her partner. Being able to separate herself from the graphic scene, she wasn't so much bothered by the blood pooled around the victim's body. For her, it was very much about the loss of life she was forced to witness.

In these cases, she'd had to deal with three lost lives in a very short span of time. Worse, she didn't know how many more bodies she'd be forced to view before the killer was stopped. The perp didn't appear to care about sex or race. Would a child be next?

Shaking her head to rid herself of that thought, she met Soames's gaze. "I wonder if, for our shooter, this victim was different somehow. Do we know how many shots yet?"

"Three, it would appear. Three shots to the chest. The trauma would have been severe. Based on the blood spatter pattern, this would have been a shot from close range as I mentioned before." Soames walked several feet in front of the body, careful to sidestep any drops of blood. "At first glance, this is where I think the shooter was. See where the blowback stops?"

Moving closer, Charli did indeed see where the back spray of blood that would have exploded toward the shooter upon impact was abruptly cut off. "Yeah, I see. Since the perp was in a car, the rest of blowback would be on his driver's side door."

Grinning at Charli as if she were a star student, Soames nodded. "We'll need to wait on more information from the blood spatter analysis, but that would be my initial guess."

It was close range then, just as the other shootings had been. Although it would be too soon for ballistics to identify whether it was a Glock 19, Charli was pretty sure it would be.

A voice came from behind Charli's back. "Detectives, I've got two witnesses waiting to speak with you."

She spun around. *Poor Officer Anderson. Even the bags under his eyes have bags.*

They were all exhausted, but at least this was a normal day on the job for Matthew and Charli. Beat cops didn't always get dispatched to three homicides in two days.

"Only two?" Matthew's right hand brushed against his receding hairline. "I thought with that crowd over there, we'd have more than that."

Officer Anderson's baby face sported a sideways frown. "Unfortunately not. Most of the shops here don't have very large windows in the front of the building, so only one witness saw what happened from inside the diner. The other was sitting in their car, waiting for a friend to arrive for lunch."

"Did either of them happen to see our gray Honda?" Charli pulled off her gloves and tossed them in a collection bin.

"Both of them. Well, the witness inside the diner only described it as a gray car." Officer Anderson shrugged. "But our other witness believes it's an Accord."

Well, that was something.

It was the first time they'd heard of a model. But since it was coming from just one victim, it wasn't enough for them to eliminate all other types. If the witness was wrong, it would leave out all other Hondas.

They met the parking lot witness first. A frazzled middle-aged woman was patting her gray bun in her rearview mirror.

"Ma'am." Charli pulled the woman's attention away from the mirror. "I'm Detective Cross, and this is my partner, Detective Church."

She extended a shaky hand toward Charli. "I'm Elizabeth Barton. Pleasure to meet you. Well, no. I suppose it isn't." Clearly doing her best to keep her composure, Elizabeth's trembling body betrayed her.

Matthew crouched down in front of her, putting a hand on the edge of her car door. "Can you tell us what you were doing here today?"

She crossed her feet at her ankles, drawing her shaking hands into her lap. "Me and a girlfriend, Mira, like to come to this diner once a week for lunch. We've been friends since high school, so we try to make time to catch up every week. But she was running late today, so I was waiting in my car for her. I just hate sitting in a diner booth alone, you know?"

Charli didn't know, actually. She'd heard people say they hated eating alone in public or visiting a movie theater by themselves. Charli had no issue with this. She could go do things by herself and be perfectly content, not that she had much time to see movies these days.

But not everyone was like her. "What happened while you were waiting?"

Elizabeth sucked in a deep breath, drawing her bottom lip between her teeth. "I didn't see the whole thing, you know. I was checking my email on my phone when, all of a sudden, I heard this horrendously loud noise. It made my entire body jump. Immediately, I started looking around, and I saw the back of this car speed off so fast that dust kicked up behind it. When the dust settled, that was when I saw the man on the ground, and the blood..." Elizabeth stared out the window in front of her, the words trailing off to a little whimper.

Charli paused for only a moment to give her time to compose herself before continuing. "And what did you do after that?"

Elizabeth reached up to smooth her hair once more, her hands continuing to shake. "I called 9-1-1 right away. I started to get out of the car to help the man, but then I remembered hearing about those other shootings." Tears brimmed in her eyes. "I realized this could be some random psycho going around shooting anybody they find, so I stayed in my car. I hope that wasn't cowardly." She put her hands in her lap once more as her chin began to quiver.

Still crouched below Charli, Matthew gave a soft smile. "No, Ms. Barton. That was smart. You've got to keep yourself safe above all. And unfortunately, the man who was shot was beyond help."

Elizabeth sucked in a long breath, nodding her head up and down. "I thought as much."

Charli leaned her shoulder atop the car door. "Can you tell us about what the car looked like?"

"It was a gray Honda Accord." The answer was immediate. "I'm positive. An old mess of a car, but my best friend had the same kind a decade ago. I'd know it anywhere. I wish I could say I got the license plate number, but everything happened so fast. I just didn't have eyes on the car that long. I'm sorry."

Charli's heart went out to the witness. Why was apologizing such a consistent theme among the witnesses they interviewed? They seemed to feel guilty for not being able to see or do more.

Rage surged through her. The asshole who had done this wasn't apologizing. He was inflicting so much trauma not only on the victim and their families but on everyone around them.

After asking Elizabeth a few more questions and exchanging contact info, they gave her the go-ahead to leave.

As the detectives strode into the diner, everyone except the witness had cleared out. Evidently, there had been a few patrons inside, but none of them had seen a thing. The only person who did was a young, sobbing waitress who sat at the shiny silver bartop.

Fiery red curls shook as the woman buried her head in her hands, tearstains on her baby blue uniform.

Charli walked up to the witness. "Lacy Mollow?"

Lacy's head shot up, her eyes wide. Bubble cheeks sat high on her heart-shaped face, her fiery hair accentuating the light green eyes that were puffy with tears.

Lacy swiped a hand across her face. "Y-yes?"

"I'm Detective Cross, and this is my partner Detective Church. We need to talk to you about the events of this afternoon."

Lacy nodded, her lower lip quivering. "I know."

Matthew and Charli sat down at a bar stool on either side of her. Lacy kept turning her head, as if she wasn't sure who to look at, but settled on Charli when she spoke up first.

"How long have you been working here, Ms. Mollow?"

"A couple years. It's my first waitressing gig, but I like it. I get a lot of nice regulars, like Roger." Tears began to stream from the corners of Lacy's eyes.

Matthew put one elbow against the countertop. "Did you know Mr. Stanton well?"

"Not really. I mean, we chatted a bit when he came in, just small talk. I knew his order by heart. He seemed like such a nice guy. And to see him like that..." Sobs racked Lacy's body, and she dropped her head in her hands once again.

Charli hated to see a witness so upset, but she had to continue questioning her. "See him like what? Can you tell us about what you saw?"

Lacy took a few heaving gasps for air, and she wiped at her tears again, this time with her sleeve. "I was standing right over there. See that stand?" She pointed to where the computer system was located a near the window. "I was putting in an order, and I saw Roger heading outside. I paused what I was doing because there was this gray car that was kind of lingering nearby. The car was a total mess. Blue tape or something on the license plate. A bunch of scratches and dents everywhere. I thought it looked out of place, but then I saw the driver..." The young woman buried her face in her hands.

Charli reached over to a napkin holder a few seats away. Pulling a few out, she offered them to Lacy. "What about the driver?"

Lacy blotted her face and blew her nose. "He had on this black mask covering most of his face. As soon as I saw that, I knew something was horribly wrong. But before I could do anything, he pulled out a gun, and...he shot Roger."

With Lacy struggling to catch her breath, Charli let her take her time. Hopefully, none of their other questions would be quite as traumatic.

They went on to ask about the model of the car, which she didn't know, and they asked her to describe the location and size of any dents. Considering how fast the event had happened, she was unsure of any exact location. Charli was thankful for what Lacy was able to recall, though she was afraid those details wouldn't help them much.

Charli finished jotting down a note. "Do you know anything about Roger's personal life? Have you ever seen him on the phone, maybe? Or talking to other diners?"

Twirling one of her curls around her finger, Lacy had sunk into a thousand-yard stare. "No. He comes in alone, and he never speaks to anyone."

"Have you ever known him to have any conflict with anyone?"

Lacy's lip began to quiver. "No, not at all. He was such a friendly guy."

After exchanging contact information with Lacy, her manager allowed her to go home. She clearly needed some space, and they'd gotten as much information as they could from her.

Once the redhead had exited, Matthew leaned against the bartop, staring at Charli. "Well, we've got a lot of the same information that reinforces what we already knew. At least Ruth will be pleased about that. What's our next move?"

"Let's get officers to search for any cameras in the area." Charli closed her eyes for a moment and drew in a deep breath. "Since he has no family we're aware of, I think we can go down to the mini-mart and speak to his employees.

Maybe they have some insight into his personal life that will guide us. But, honestly, Matt, I think the best thing for us to start doing is manually going through every single streetlight camera that is even remotely in the area of these shootings. We can get a couple officers to help us."

Matthew let out a long groan. "I can't even fathom how long that's going to take. And you're right. We're going to have to enlist some help."

Charli picked up the crumpled napkins Lacy had left before standing. "Yeah, it's going to require more manpower, but this is getting out of hand fast. Ruth is right. The public is going to be losing their minds. We need to put all available resources on this case."

Matthew pulled out his phone. "Yeah, okay. Why don't we call Ruth now?"

Even before he pulled up his contacts, Charli's phone rang. She tapped the speaker button. "Detective Cross speaking."

"This is Officer Ryland. I'm driving southbound on Elm Street, approaching Fourth Avenue. I'm following a gray Honda Accord. Looks to be from around 1997."

"Pull it over." Heart racing, Charli headed toward the door. "We can be there in five. Keep the occupants until we get there."

Though she told herself to stay calm, that there were plenty of gray Hondas in Savannah, just the possibility that this could be the car had her heart soaring.

"Not a problem. I'll tell him I'm pulling him over because his license plate isn't visible."

Charli's heart took another leap. "Wait, why can't you see the license plate?"

"There's some kind of tarp covering the back plate."

Bingo.

"Don't mention the license plate. You'll need to find another excuse. And whatever you do, don't say anything about that tarp." She exchanged a glance with Matthew before continuing. "And Officer?"

"Yeah?"

"Be careful."

16

C harli came in on two wheels as she parked behind Officer Ryland's squad car. Well, it was Charli's version of speeding at least. In the passenger seat, Matthew yawned.

Fine. Maybe two wheels was a bit of an exaggeration, but could anyone really blame her?

She was an officer of the law, after all, and if she didn't obey traffic laws, how could she expect the public to do the same? More importantly, she was always careful not to go too fast even when she was in a hurry because she knew that vehicle accidents and assaults caused nine out of ten line-of-duty fatalities. Charli didn't want to end up as part of that statistic. She had too many bad guys to catch.

"Matt!" She was out of her car in an instant, craning her neck to get a better view of the Honda in question. "Do you see that?"

Matthew snorted. "How could I not see it? It looks like some kind of blue tarp over the license plate."

Officer Ryland nodded as they approached but kept his eyes on the driver. Charli couldn't make out the person in great detail, but the man had his hands on the steering wheel where she was sure he'd been ordered to keep them.

"What do we have, Officer?"

Ryland tipped his hat to her. "The driver's name is Lance Raken. I did as you suggested and didn't mention the license plate. Instead, I let him know he'd been speeding, which is true. He's been waiting on me to run his driver's license. The man has no priors. He's clean as a whistle."

Matthew came around the side of the car, his hand on his firearm. "Well, let's make sure that's the case."

Charli had her own hand on her holster. If this was their guy, there was a chance this interaction could get violent fast. "Has he been compliant with you so far? Have you noticed any agitation?"

Ryland, an officer in his thirties, ran his hands over his protruding beer belly. His fingers twitched. "Nope. He seems real calm, but I suppose that could be an act."

Charli nodded. "Thank you, Officer. Be ready to call for backup."

Charli and Matthew moved to the driver's side door, which was wide open. When they reached Lance's peripherals, his hands moved off his steering wheel and into his lap.

"Sir, please keep your hands on the wheel."

Matthew's command voice had the driver gripping the wheel before the words were completely out of his mouth. "Yes, sir."

Looking nervous as hell, Lance glanced at Charli, as if she might be the sympathetic one of the pair. Didn't his mama tell him to not judge a book by its cover?

"Ma'am, I'm not—"

Charli pulled her badge. "That's Detective Cross to you, Mr. Raken."

The jittery smile the driver was attempting to hold in

place fell away. "Detective? Why does a speeding stop need a detective?" He shrugged with his hands.

"Sir," Matthew's command voice was even louder this time, "we need you to keep your hands where we can see them."

Lance's bushy brown eyebrows furrowed, but he complied. "Okay, I guess. I gotta say, this is the weirdest traffic stop I've ever experienced."

"Mr. Raken. I'm sure you've heard, but the city is on high alert right now." Resting her hand just above her gun, her voice oozed a calm she didn't quite feel.

Lance's face softened, concern in his eyes. "You're talking about those shootings? So tragic. I've been on edge all day. You guys any closer to finding the guy?"

Either he's genuinely concerned, or he's one hell of an actor.

Charli ignored the question. "Since you're familiar with the case, are you aware of the type of vehicle in question?"

It took a couple of seconds, but Lance's eyes finally widened. "A gray Honda, right?" He glanced around the interior of his car as if seeing it for the first time. "Like mine?"

Give that man a prize.

"That's correct, sir. A gray Honda with a concealed licensed plate."

With a little laugh, Lance relaxed into his seat, though he kept his hands tight on the steering wheel. "Then that's clearly not me. Whew. Scared me a little bit there."

Charli maintained her calm demeanor, not willing to be taken in by what very well could be an innocent act. "Mr. Raken, do we have permission to search you and your vehicle?"

The man's double take would have been amusing under any other circumstance. "Search my car?" He shook his head like a dog after a bath. "Why?"

Charli was getting tired of this. "Because your license plate is concealed."

Lance whipped his head around, as if he could see the back of his car that way. "What? No, it isn't."

"Mr. Raken, would you like to see for yourself?" When he reached for his seat belt, she lifted a hand. "Stop!" He froze in place, and Charli walked him through the process of getting out of his vehicle without causing alarm. "With your right hand only, unbuckle your belt, keeping your left hand where we can see it."

With precisely measured steps, Charli provided instructions until the driver was outside of his vehicle and had moved to the trunk area. Matthew and the officer moved to either side of the car, their eyes never leaving the suspect.

He was a stout man, not morbidly overweight, but stocky and with a good bit of muscle on his arms. With his short buzzed brown hair, he gave Charli the impression of a bulldog.

Hands held at shoulder height, Lance stared at the tarp covering his license plate. His face drained of color, and he turned to Charli. "I...I-I didn't know. I've got several tarps in my trunk right now."

Alarm bells rang in Charli's head. "Why do you have multiple tarps in your vehicle?"

"I run my own painting business. Just started, actually." Lance's eyebrows rose high on his forehead. "Used to be a painter with a bigger company, but I've been striking out on my own to do odd jobs here and there. If you know anyone in need of a painter, I can give you my card."

Charli went back to her original question. "Mind if we take a look? Do we have permission to search you and your vehicle?"

With zero hesitation this time, Lance nodded furiously. "Of course. Do anything you need to do."

Glancing at Officer Ryland to make sure his body cam was pointed in their direction, Charli relaxed knowing the approval had been caught on camera. "Sir, do you have any weapons on your person or in your vehicle? Or anything sharp that might harm us during our search?"

Lance shook his head. "Nothing at all, but I do have some small tools in the trunk. Putty knives, paintbrushes, that kind of thing."

At her nod, Officer Ryland stepped forward. "Sir, please place your hands on the back of the car and spread your legs." After a thorough pat down that resulted in finding nothing more than a pocket full of change and a stick of chewing gum, they all relaxed a little.

"Mr. Raken, I'm going to open your trunk. Do I still have permission to do so?"

"Yes. Of course."

"May I retrieve your keys from the ignition?" After another quick nod, Charli did exactly that. "Thank you for your cooperation. We'll be as quick as we can."

At the start of her career as a beat cop, Charli would occasionally find it uncomfortable to be forceful with individuals when she had no idea if they were guilty or not. Lance, for example, was a pretty friendly guy. But Charli no longer had any qualms about putting people like him through the wringer when it came to matters of safety. Offending an innocent was better than giving a criminal the opportunity to hurt someone, including herself.

As Charli retrieved the keys, Matthew kept his post beside Lance, his hand never far away from his gun on his hip.

While Matthew kept his eyes on Lance, Charli motioned for Officer Ryland to assist her as she walked around the car to the trunk. Gloving up, she waited until the officer had done the same.

Taking a deep breath, she inserted the key into the trunk. *Here goes nothing...or everything.* Being such an old car, it wasn't terribly easy to get the lock to pop open. Charli had to jiggle it considerably. With every second that passed, her heart threatened to explode out of her damn chest.

After a few moments of finagling, the lock clicked, and the trunk lid began to rise.

Tarps...so many tarps. *Lance wasn't kidding.*

After setting not three or four but seven tarps aside, Charli watched as Ryland did a thorough search of the trunk, revealing a few sealed paint cans along with rollers, pans stained with white paint, and various hand tools. He even opened the cans, using a stir stick to swirl the contents.

Nothing.

Relief mixed with disappointment. *He sure doesn't seem to be our killer. But if he's not our guy, the psycho is still out there.*

While Officer Ryland continued to conduct a thorough search, Charli approached Matthew and Lance. His arms were beginning to sag. "Can you tell me about your day? Please go through everything that's happened since you woke this morning."

Before he could respond, Matthew directed him to sit on the curb. Seemingly grateful for the change, Lance tucked his knees together as he sat down. "Woke up pretty early to paint a client's living room. Probably around six a.m. I've been there all day, with the exception of dropping by the local deli for some lunch." Lance shrugged, causing his stained red plaid shirt to rise up and wrinkle.

Charli pulled out her notebook. "Can anyone confirm that?"

"Sure." Lance's tone had become more cheerful. How he'd managed to be pleasant through this ordeal was beyond Charli, but it was a solid reminder that there were many more good people in her city than bad. "My business partner, Ricky Lennar. I can give you his number now, if you want."

After jotting down the contact information and having Officer Ryland run it to make sure it was legitimate, Charli dialed the number. As Lance had declared, Ricky recounted his day in the same exact way that Lance had.

He's just a man with a beat-up Honda Accord.

After disconnecting the call, Charli stuck her hand out, offering the still-seated man an assist to standing. "I want to thank you, Mr. Raken, for not only your cooperation but for being so pleasant as we did what we needed to do."

Lance dusted off the seat of his pants and smiled, though it seemed more wistful this time. "Stop every Honda Accord that you think you need to, Detective. Stop this asshole however you can."

His understanding caused Charli's eyes to burn, and she blinked away the sudden rush of emotion. "We're going to do just that. Again, thank you for your cooperation. Have a nice rest of your day."

After watching their cooperative person of interest drive away and thanking Officer Ryland for his support, Charli turned to Matthew. "That was both good and bad."

Matthew seemed to understand. "Good human being, but now we're back to the drawing board, huh?" Matthew let out a low whistle. "Between you and me, I was really hoping it was him. That this case was over."

"Me too. But since it's not..." Charli pulled her cell phone from her pocket.

Matthew gave her a sideways glance. "What are you doing?"

"Calling Ruth. If that wasn't our guy, we need to tell her that we need more people on the case."

Matthew groaned. "She's going to love that."

True, their sergeant wasn't going to be thrilled that they

were no closer to finding a connection between these three murders, but she would appreciate that they were trying their best to throw everything they had at the case.

"Please tell me you've got something good, Cross."

Charli exchanged a glance with Matthew. *He looks as disappointed as I feel.*

"Not so much, but what I do have is a plan. Matthew and I want to start searching all the streetlight cameras to see if we can get a path on the Accord. But we're going to need some more manpower to do it."

Ruth was quiet for a moment, keeping Charli and Matthew on the edge of their seats.

"If you need more manpower, you're going to be very happy to hear that help has been secured."

Reading her sergeant's tone, Charli glanced at Matthew. *He isn't going to like this.*

As if on cue, Matthew slapped his palm to his forehead. "Sergeant, please don't tell me what I think you're going to tell me."

"Be grateful for the extra help, Detective Church. Yes, the FBI is taking over the case."

17

I loathed the fluorescent lights of the doctor's office. They made the sterile white walls even more blinding than they normally were.

Why the hell was I even here? What was the point? Didn't I already know everything I needed to?

I'd considered skipping this appointment, and normally, I would have, but I had to be more careful than ever not to raise red flags, especially today of all days. Ridding the world of two more lying, useless people was better than I could have hoped for, and having a regularly scheduled doctor's appointment then canceling at the last minute might be considered a red flag.

Maybe.

But why take any chances when I had to appear as normal as possible.

My mission wasn't finished quite yet.

Though I hated to admit it, there was one nice thing about coming to the doctor today. I wasn't quite as bored out of my freaking mind. A quiet, elderly woman with her nose stuck in a magazine was across from me. She was the only other person here besides the receptionist clacking away at the keyboard behind the front desk.

"They don't know what you've done."

Damian was right.

Neither of them knew they were currently in the same room with the man who the media had called a monster. They had no idea that I'd ended two lives today.

Nobody had a clue about the control I held, the sheer power.

Excitement bubbled up inside me like a drug. I was good at this. Why hadn't I stepped up a long time ago? Why had I wasted all those years?

All the time I could have spent picking off these useless assholes...wasted.

"Better late than never."

Damian twisted my guts with the reminder, making me groan. Fighting through the pain, I thought of a cliché of my own..."Live each day as if it were your last."

Plenty of men had tried to claim the quote, but I knew better. Roman Emperor Marcus Aurelius had pronounced it two millennia ago.

It had served him well. And now, I was doing the same thing.

My only regret was that it had taken me so long to take the blinders off. Before now, my life was meaningless. It had been so rigid and so...moral. I cringed at the thought.

What was the point in trying to be good? To have morals and values and blah blah blah. All they did was suck all the fun from life.

Now, I had a secret anywhere I went. Nothing would ever be mundane again. Anytime I looked into someone's eyes, I thought about how I was capable of closing those eyes forever.

The TV in the corner of the room had been playing a

commercial about laundry detergent a moment ago, complete with a dachshund puppy hopping into a pile of fresh white sheets. It had shifted, though, and the evening news was playing.

I turned in my seat to get a better view of the screen, pain shooting up through my lower back as I did. I ignored it.

"And the Savannah serial sniper seems to have struck again. This morning, we told you about a shooting at a local bus stop. We can now announce that the victim was local x-ray technician Gretta Franklin."

The perky blonde anchor kept a straight face as an image of Gretta popped up on the screen. They'd picked a photo of her in her scrubs, grinning from ear to ear. Leave it to the newshounds to try to make that bitch look like a sweetheart.

How disgusting.

Why did the media always do this shit? Why did they portray someone as a saint just because they no longer stole the air that the rest of us needed to breathe?

Not every victim was actually a victim. Hell, most murder victims weren't good. A lot of them had been killed for good reasons. And yet, I could end the life of the biggest scumbag, and they'd become a saint in the local papers.

The camera panned to a male anchor. *"Unfortunately, since Gretta's death, yet another shooting has taken place. A male in his forties was shot outside of a local diner. We'll go to Mark, who is on the scene."*

A torrent of emotions swirled inside me as Mark droned on about my most recent accomplishment. At the forefront of those emotions was sheer pride. They called me evil. A monster. A despicable killer. Those assholes should be thanking me instead.

"Just don't get caught."

With those few words, Damian stirred up a hurricane of anxiety in my chest. With every new shooting, the chances of getting caught increased. I'd been incredibly lucky so far, but I simply didn't have the time or energy to plan each riddance as meticulously as I wanted to.

But I wasn't stupid. I knew I'd be caught eventually. The whole city was in an uproar, and no doubt the FBI was involved or would be soon. Being caught wasn't what bothered me. Hell, when I finished, maybe I would just turn myself in.

On second thought, maybe I'd just keep killing until I keeled over one day. After all, my lust for vengeance only continued to grow.

As did my smile.

I knew I must look like an idiot grinning like that, but I didn't give a damn what anyone thought. That ship had sailed.

"We're ready for you now, sir." The receptionist waved with her perfectly manicured nails.

Not that those perfect nails helped make her more attractive. On the contrary, the manicure only made her look more ridiculous. She was a woman in her forties with an awful maroon dye job barely covering her gray roots, the filler in her lips giving her a hideous duckface. Everything about her was fake.

Even worse, all those cosmetic procedures cost a fortune. How many people had come in here unable to pay their medical bills? Meanwhile, this uppity receptionist could afford Botox.

Come to think of it, this woman should've made my list. Hell, before it was over, maybe I'd add her name. But I couldn't destroy every immoral person in Savannah. I had to be selective and focus on those who had wronged me the most...

Like the doctor waiting on the other side of that door.

Pushing to my feet, my breath quickened from both pain

and excitement as I pulled the door open. Would he know? Would he be able to see the new cancer growing inside me? Would he see Damian?

Just a glimpse of his gleaming smile was enough of an answer. Of course he didn't see my little friend. The quack actually hadn't seen the initial cancerous growth until it had sunk its killer fangs into my blood stream. Why was I expecting anything different today?

"So good to see you again." His teeth sparkled under the blinding fluorescent lighting. Although he was most certainly also in his forties, he had aged a lot better than the receptionist.

I hated him for it. Hated those perfect cheekbones. His full, lush hairline. Real doctors shouldn't look like they came out of an episode of *Grey's Anatomy*.

And why the hell would he say that to me? Didn't he even think before he spoke? He should know damn well that it was not good to see him. What was I supposed to say to that? I wasn't going to lie anymore. I'd decided that as soon as I started the list. No more social niceties.

Prick.

When I said nothing, he turned around to wash his hands in the sink. "Anything I need to know since our last visit?" The smile was still present in his voice.

What a perfect opportunity. Anytime I came in for a checkup, he always had to wash his hands. There was a vulnerability in a person turning their back. For all his wealth and good looks, this doctor was no man. A real man would know not to leave their back open to his enemy.

Especially not someone who hated everything they stood for.

Couldn't he feel my rage?

"Just kill him now while you have the chance."

"You know I can't do that yet, Damian." My voice came

out a whisper, and Dr. I-Don't-Give-a-Shit-What-Happens-to-My-Patients didn't even turn around.

"You may not get another opportunity like this."

My head was spinning as fast as the center of a tornado, and I clamped my hands over my ears, willing the whirlwind to stop.

"Are you okay?"

How dare this man pretend to be concerned about me now. Once the dizziness began to subside, I shook his hand off my shoulder. "Just peachy."

The bastard grinned at my sarcasm, and I itched to wipe that phony smile off his face. Reaching into my pocket, my fingertips brushed over the smooth edges of the coins I carried. Just that touch provided a soothing balm for the rage coursing through my veins.

Only three were left.

Lucky for him, he wasn't next on my list. It wouldn't be long now, though.

His time would come.

18

Matthew rested his head on the seat as Charli pulled into the precinct parking lot. "You have got to be kidding me. Could this day get any worse?"

News vans lined the entrance to the precinct. Matthew should have expected this, but he'd been too focused on the fact that his case now involved a babysitter.

"It's not that big of a deal." Charli shrugged. "We can just take the back entrance. They won't bother us."

While that was true, the news vans being present had far bigger implications. "They're going to bother Serg, that's for sure. She's going to be all over our asses. And now we have to coordinate with the FBI *and* the GBI?"

Matthew could read Charli's mind before she even answered. He had no clue why, but working with the Feds never seemed to bother her much.

Charli's apple cheeks protruded farther when she half-smiled at Matthew. "Look, we really do need the resources. They can provide them. And as much as I hate to admit it, this case is getting out of hand. We've got no leads, three dead people, and no obvious connections. And when someone else dies, who is the public looking to? Us. Do you really want to hold all the blame for not finding this guy?"

That wasn't what it was about, though. Yes, of course they needed the resources, and he'd always considered himself a team player. But the fact that they hadn't been able to solve this case on their own drove him crazy.

This was more than just a matter of the Feds stepping in to help. Not too long ago, his wife had divorced him and taken his daughter all the way out to California. Even worse, another man had stepped in and taken his place. Now, yet another person would be taking over the case that he hadn't been able to make heads or tails of so far.

Charli was right, though. This case was far too big. People were dying daily. If the news vans were any indication, the public was living in a state of constant fear. They had to get to the bottom of this, preferably yesterday, as Ruth would say.

Matthew winced and gave himself a mental shake.

After they sneaked through the back of the building and into the main hall, a familiar voice rang out from behind them.

"Charli! Long time, no see."

Matthew didn't need to turn around to know who it was. Of course the GBI agent assigned to their case was none other than Preston Powell.

Something about the guy just irked Matthew, and it had been that way since their first case together. This time, though, something was different, but he couldn't quite put his finger on it.

Matthew wasn't a master of body language, but he could have sworn Charli's entire body was saying...run.

Why?

A while back, Powell had asked Charli out on a date. She had agreed, but to Matthew's intense consternation, she'd never shared the outcome. Based on the forced smile plastered on his partner's face, it hadn't gone too well.

Charli thrust out her hand. "Agent Powell, great to see you."

Confusion blipped across Powell's face, but it disappeared as fast as it came. Although Charli either didn't seem to notice the look or ignored it, Matthew hadn't missed it. He also hadn't missed his partner's formal greeting of the GBI agent.

And what was Matthew, chopped liver? Not that he minded so much. If Powell didn't want to greet him, he was perfectly fine not offering a greeting back.

Taking her hand in his, Powell's gaze swept from her feet to her hair. "I was just about to head to your office."

Whoa there, buddy. Nothing to see here. Keep your eyes on her face.

Although Matthew had no doubt Charli could take care of herself, it still ticked him off that the jackass had checked out his partner.

Hell, if it had been Chelsea instead of Charli, Matthew would have come unglued in a heartbeat. He forced that thought out of his head. The last thing he needed to worry about was some teenage punk getting up close and personal with his daughter, especially when she was across the country and there was nothing he could do about it. Besides, he had a case that needed his utmost attention.

"Have you been briefed on the case? Because, if not, Sergeant Morris likely wants to speak to you." Though he was bristling, Matthew kept the irritation from his voice. As much as he disliked Powell, he wasn't about to make this investigation awkward by showing him any overt animosity.

He was eager to delay them having to work together, though. And if Ruth still needed to brief Powell, that would give Matthew a bit of time to psych himself up for it.

"We already spoke, but I'm looking forward to digging down into the details with you two."

Yeah, I'll bet you are.

When they reached their office, Matthew took a seat as Charli headed to the murder board to add the information about their latest victim. Powell made himself comfortable in one of the chairs that usually collected dust in the corner of the room.

"Has Sergeant Morris told you that we plan to start going through as many streetlight cameras as we possibly can?" Charli knitted her brows, causing a little wrinkle to form between them. "Because we need your team on that with us as soon as possible."

"Of course. Cyber security is already getting that footage pulled." Powell removed an iPad from his briefcase. "I heard you applied for a warrant to obtain a list of Gretta Franklin's patients. What's the status on that?"

"We know it's a long shot that a judge will give us the records, but with these extenuating circumstances, we're hoping to get it signed." Charli strode across the room and sat down at her computer. "I can check right now to see if we've got a stamp of approval."

Her fingertips were tapping away at her keyboard when Ruth walked in, scribbling something on a notepad as soon as she stopped walking. There was no way her handwriting was legible at the speed she was jotting things down.

As long as she can read it, that's all that matters.

"I see you have reacquainted yourself with Agent Powell." Ruth glanced up, sweeping a sharp gaze across the room. "Good. Makes my life a little easier."

Charli nodded toward the notebook in Ruth's hand. "What's that?"

"I'm about to give a press conference, and I'm hoping you might have an update that makes me not look incompetent in front of a horde of reporters." The sergeant's brown eyes fixed on each person in the room. "Any links between our victims that might suggest that these killings are not random?"

Charli bit her bottom lip. "We don't have anything yet, but—"

"Great." Ruth threw up her arms. "So, basically, I need to go out and tell these reporters that for all we know, the killer is targeting random people and that anyone could be a victim."

Uh oh.

Whenever their sergeant pulled out her sarcasm, she was stressed to the max. Matthew exchanged a glance with Charli, but he didn't dare mouth anything, afraid that Ruth would notice. He'd already gotten caught in the act while impersonating her and was pretty sure he was walking on thin ice with the way the sergeant's mood was right now.

As Ruth pinned Charli with her stare, a man walked up behind her. Built like a wrestler and dressed in black from his button-down to his pristine boots, he had short black hair cropped close to his head. Light brown eyes contrasted with his smooth ebony skin.

He cleared his throat. "I would be surprised if that were true. If these murders were random, we would see some pattern of convenience. With Victor Layne and Gretta Franklin's death, I'd be able to believe that our killer saw something convenient about finding two people alone before the sun rose. But with our latest murder taking place in the middle of the day with people around, it suggests Roger Stanton was a defined target."

The man didn't even bother introducing himself. "You are?" Matthew didn't mean the question to sound aggressive in the slightest, but the Fed still snapped his head toward him with narrowed eyes.

"I'm Special Agent Jay Brady. I'll be the FBI lead on this case. The GBI team is here to offer us more heads on the case as well."

At least he didn't indicate that he was taking over the case. That was something.

While Matthew appreciated the extra resources the FBI was able to provide, this was the part he didn't like. He and Charli were no longer going to run their own case in the way they saw fit.

Matthew couldn't deny that, ultimately, this FBI agent was bringing invaluable experience to their team. Even more importantly, this guy seemed knowledgeable about drive-bys.

Still, it sucked that Mr. Know-It-All would be calling all the shots.

Ruth gave a curt nod. "Thank you, Agent Brady. I hope you don't mind if I use that line of thinking during my speech to the press."

Agent Brady turned his head toward Ruth, but his expression remained solemn. "No problem at all. Whatever we have to do to keep the public calm. The last thing we need is the entire city in a panic."

Charli cleared her throat. "Well, Agent Brady, we're happy to have you on board. If there's anything we can do to be of help, we'll be glad to do it."

The agent didn't move a muscle. Was this man a robot? Had they switched the FBI over to artificial intelligence or something?

"Thank you, Detective Cross." Even with his mouth moving, the rest of his face remained still. "I think the first point of order is going to be you and your partner seeking out Roger Stanton's mini-mart and interviewing his employees. We're still looking for any close friends or family members, but he appears to be a lone wolf. Perhaps his employees will have some insight into his personal life."

Hot damn.

As randomly assigned tasks went, this one wasn't too bad. It sure beat going through the street camera footage.

Charli nodded as she reached for her keys. "I'd be happy to head out there. I was just going to check to see if the warrant for Gretta Franklin's patient list got approved, and then we'll head that way."

Brady held up a hand. "We'll be handling warrant requests and approvals moving forward. Anything that can be handled in the office, my team will work on it right away. But I'd love to use your interview skills in the field, Detective. Of course, we'll update you as soon as we get approval."

Charli didn't seem to mind one bit. A small smile tugged at her lips. "That sounds fantastic. Thank you."

Matthew wished he shared his partner's happy attitude.

19

"Of course I'm happy." Charli shot Matthew an *are you shitting me* glance as they pulled into the mini-mart parking lot. "Do you know how much I hate paperwork?"

One of the things she loved most about being a detective was getting out in the field. Sure, she also liked going over data back at the precinct. Using her analysis skills was also a perk of the job.

But the one thing she loathed was filling out requests for information and making phone calls where she had to deal with government bureaucrats.

Matthew scowled as he flung the passenger door shut. "Yeah, I guess."

She walked around the front of her car. "Seriously, Matt. Just let them handle the parts of our case that are mind-numbing."

Charli would never understand how Matthew could be so resistant to receiving help from the Feds, especially under these circumstances. As talented as Charli believed she was as a detective, there was no denying that a case like this could become overwhelming fast. The entire city was relying on them to find this killer. Now, they had some help with that suffocating burden.

The OPEN sign outside the mini-mart had been turned off, but there was still someone behind the counter. A younger man with long blond hair that curled around his ears was intent on some kind of task.

Charli pulled the door's handle, surprised that it was unlocked.

The young man didn't even glance up as he continued drawing something she couldn't quite see. Charli peered over the counter where the kid was writing in graffiti style, his head bent low as he worked on the shading.

It was a sign. "Closed Until Further Notice."

Charli knocked on the counter. "Hello…?"

The young man's head jerked up, causing his blond locks to rise and fall as he yelped in surprise. "Sh…sorry. I thought the door was locked." As he glanced between the two of them, Charli spotted earbuds in his ears.

She smiled to set his mind at ease and tapped her own ear, silently asking him to remove the buds. "It's okay. I'm Detective Cross. My partner, Detective Church, and I would like to talk to you about your boss, Roger Stanton."

He glanced back down at his sign. "Sure, what can I help you with?"

"Can you tell us your full name please?"

The young man picked up a badge that had been tossed onto the counter. "David," was all it said. When Charli lifted an eyebrow, he blushed. "Sorry. Abby. David Abby."

Matthew took a few steps toward the counter. "David, we were hoping you could tell us about the last time you spoke to Mr. Stanton."

"Today. Just forty-five minutes or so before…it happened. But he didn't say much, just that he'd be back in an hour." He dropped his gaze to the floor, the weariness evident in his hazel eyes.

Charli could imagine what a shock it was to hear of his employer's sudden passing, especially in such a brutal way. "How long did you work for Mr. Stanton?"

He rummaged under the counter, producing a roll of tape. "About two years. He hired me when I was eighteen."

"In that two years, did you two grow close?" It was a yes or no question, but sometimes a quick answer provided more information than a hundred words ever could.

Charli was right.

David rolled his eyes and chuckled, a ghost of a smile on his face. "I'm sorry. It's an inappropriate time to laugh, I know. I do that sometimes. But, no, we were anything but close. The guy got on my nerves a lot. He's my boss, ya know? And he was kind of an obnoxious boss at that, but he definitely didn't deserve this."

Charli pulled out her notepad and continued on with the basic introductory questions before getting to the one she was most eager to learn the answer to. "Do you know of anyone who disliked Mr. Stanton?"

As unlikely as it was, Charli couldn't dismiss the idea that someone might piggyback on a situation like this to cover up their own murder. After all, what better time to kill an enemy than when a random shooter was on the loose?

David shrugged, causing his button-down navy-blue shirt to rise and fall. "Me and my coworker, I guess. And plenty of people who came in with a complaint about the store. Small shit like they grabbed an expired candy bar or something. Mr. Stanton wasn't so great about taking complaints and it could get kinda heated."

Charli and Matthew exchanged a glance before Matthew asked, "Can you think of anyone specifically?"

"Nah." David strode over to the front door and propped it

open, taping the sign up for potential customers. "They weren't any big fights or threats, if that's what you're looking for. Not big enough to go shoot him over. If anyone had a personal problem with Mr. Stanton, I didn't know about it. He kept his personal life separate from work."

Charli glanced up at the sign as the door swung shut. "No estimate of when you guys will be opened up again, huh?"

David let out a long sigh. "As far as I'm aware, I just lost my job. Mr. Stanton owned this place, and he didn't have any family who worked with him. Not sure who's going to inherit the store, but it'll probably take weeks to figure it out. And I doubt they'll bring me or Kyle back."

"What's Kyle's last name?" Matthew's gaze followed David as he walked back around the counter.

"Jessup." David ran his hands through the sides of his hair.

Charli tapped her pen against her notepad. "We're going to need his contact information."

"Yeah, no worries. I can give it to you now. I sent him home a while ago, told him I didn't need him to close up shop. But he worked today too."

That was going to be Charli's next question. And if Kyle disliked his employer as much as David, Charli had to check into that. "Where were you and Kyle at the time of the shooting?"

"We were both here in the store. We were waiting for Mr. Stanton to come back to give us our breaks. When he didn't show up, we knew something wasn't right. The dude was an asshole, but he ran this place with an iron fist. He was always on time." The kid said it like being punctual was a bad thing.

Charli steered him back on course. "What happened when he didn't arrive?"

"We kept calling him, and eventually, a police officer answered to tell us what was going on." David put his elbow on the counter, letting his chin fall into his hand. "It's weird, ya know? I didn't exactly like him, but it's hard to know he's just gone from this world. Like, it can be any of us at any time."

Oh, how Charli was aware.

The one thing this case had done for her was put Madeline mostly out of her head, but after David's comment, thoughts of her friend resurfaced. Before the teen's death, Charli didn't think much of her own mortality. After Madeline died, it was all she thought about.

Death just wasn't something one conceptualized until it happened to a loved one. Or, in David's case, it happened to someone he disliked. But still, Charli's heart went out to the kid. He was young, and this was likely his first brush with death.

Matthew pointed to a security camera in the corner of the store. "Does it work?"

"That dinosaur?" David straightened his posture, a hint of a smile on his face. "As ancient as it is, it still works. Mr. Stanton said it was to cut down on any potential theft, but I think he just wanted to keep tabs on me and Kyle when he wasn't here. We knew better than to get into any trouble, though. Would you like to see the tape?"

Matthew flashed him a smile. "We certainly would."

After reviewing the footage and confirming David and Kyle's alibi, Charli had run out of questions to ask.

"Are you guys any closer to catching this g-guy?" David's voice cracked on the last word. "I don't mean to sound like a coward or anything, but even just walking to my car is stressing me out. The news reports say these are all random shootings. It could be any one of us."

Charli forced a smile. "I promise we're doing our best, and we're working with the FBI and GBI to solve this case as fast as we can. We'd be happy to walk you to your car, though, to provide a little extra reassurance."

David seemed to consider this for a moment, then shook his head. "Nah. I'm being paranoid."

Matthew shifted his weight to one leg. "Not at all. You're just being sensible. Do you live by yourself?"

David waved his hands around, motioning at the shelves around him. "Dude, I work at a shitty little mini-mart. Do you think I can afford my own place?"

Matthew grinned. "Well, then, allow us to make sure you get back home to your parents safe. I'm sure they're worried after hearing about your boss."

David made an "uhm" sound before nodding. "Okay, sure, for my parents. But just to my car is fine."

After getting both David and Kyle's contact information, the young man locked up the small store, and the detectives escorted him to a banged up vehicle...a red Mustang that looked to be on its last two legs.

When he drove off, Charli glanced at her notes. "We could head over to Kyle's house now and ask him some questions."

But Matthew seemed to be a million miles away. "I'm glad Chelsea isn't in Savannah right now. I can't believe I'm saying it, and I never thought I would, but at least I don't have to worry about her during all this. I'd never be able to focus on this case if I thought some random shooter was running around. It would be hard not to spend every minute trying to protect my family."

"In all likelihood, it's not a random shooter, according to Agent Brady." Charli wasn't sure why she said this. She knew that wasn't Matthew's point.

When he only nodded along half-heartedly, Charli gave Matthew a quick pat on the shoulder. "I'm glad she's safe too."

Matthew smiled down at her. "Thanks, Charli. Now, let's

go speak to Kyle. We don't want the FBI breathing down the poor kid's neck. Wait, do robots breathe?"

"Robots?" Charli raised her eyebrows as she walked around to her car door. "What are you talking about?"

"Oh, did I not tell you? Agent Brady is a government created robot. He was made to assist on serial murders."

As corny as he could be, Charli loved her partner. "Oh, shut up."

She couldn't deny it, though. Agent Brady did give her robot vibes.

"What?" Matthew shrugged, the picture of innocence. "It wasn't an insult. Robots can be very helpful, you know."

Charli raised her eyebrows. "They can, huh?"

"Sure. Haven't you ever seen *The Terminator*?" Matthew drew himself up to his full height and puffed out his chest. "I'llll be baaack."

That was enough to send Charli into a fit of laughter, and Matthew chuckled along with her. This was the kind of humor they needed.

But when the laughter stopped, the darkness of their case was still there, and they weren't any closer to finding the person terrorizing their city.

20

"What's that?" Stopped at a red light, Charli glanced away from the wheel for a moment to get a peek at what Matthew was watching on his phone. To Charli's ears, it was just random chatter, but Matthew wasn't one to leisurely play videos while at work.

"It's a replay of the serg's press conference. Here, I'll turn it up."

Ruth's firm, decisive words filled the car's airspace.

I know the citizens of Savannah are fearful, but we are using all our resources while working on this case. Savannah is fortunate to have some of the country's finest detectives, and we're now partnering with the FBI and GBI as we explore every avenue to bring the killer to justice.

If you have witnessed anything that you think may be helpful in our investigation, please don't hesitate to contact us as we work around the clock to apprehend the person or persons committing these terrible acts. We've established a dedicated tip line where you can call twenty-four-seven. The number is...

"Wow, I don't think she's ever sounded that warm and

caring when she's speaking to us." Charli couldn't prevent the grin from spreading across her face.

Matthew snickered. "Nah, she's usually barking out orders. But hey, she keeps us in line, doesn't she? I can't think of anyone else I'd rather work under."

Charli agreed.

Sergeant Ruth Morris never failed to impress Charli with her ability to speak to the citizens of Savannah with such compassion and poise. She doubted that she'd be able to do it herself. Charli might be a fantastic detective, but she didn't have the disposition or the desire to deal with the press on a regular basis.

She turned into the parking lot of the precinct. "Hopefully, this will help calm some of the panic in the city."

"I wouldn't hold my breath. I don't think anything is going to calm the citizens of Savannah except finding this killer. Or, if we don't, then we'll need a fair amount of time to pass before people forget about it."

"We're going to find this bastard." Charli slammed her fist against the dash and turned to face her partner. "With every new victim, our killer reveals more about themself. We're close. I can feel it."

Matthew pushed his car door open. "There's a couple problems with that, you know?"

Charli deflated. "Yeah, I know. I don't want anyone else to die, but unless we have another victim, we're stuck spinning around, trying to find this shooter with only the lack of evidence we currently have."

Climbing out of her car, Charli forced away the gnawing sensation in the pit of her stomach.

If nobody else lost their lives to this lunatic, that would be ideal. Charli would have no complaints if nobody else died, but the idea that this person could kill three people and get away with it was too much.

She prided herself on her rate of solved cases. She didn't like to let even one case slip through the cracks. That reminded her too much of Madeline and the fact that her killer was never held accountable. For Charli, an unsolved murder was personal.

As they entered the precinct, Special Agent Jay Brady's boots stomped against the white tile of the lobby to meet Charli and Matthew. "Detective Cross. Detective Church. I wanted to make sure you knew that the warrant has come back, and the hospital was super responsive. You'll find a list of Gretta Franklin's patients in your email."

Charli released a breath of air she'd been holding for the past forty-eight hours. "That's the best news we've heard all day. Thank you, Agent Brady."

Perhaps the murderer didn't need to shoot anyone else for them to narrow down the details of their identity. A small weight tumbled from Charli's shoulders, but the reprieve was short-lived.

Agent Brady tugged at his collar, making the muscles in his arm more pronounced. "I'm afraid we've already cross-referenced them with our list of Glock 19 and Honda owners. We don't have a match."

How can he deliver that kind of news without so much as lifting an eyebrow? Impressive.

Charli couldn't help but experience a twinge of envy. Showing such little emotion in high-stress situations was certainly a gift.

Her heart sank down into her stomach. Charli had been so hopeful that Gretta's list of patients would give them the lead they needed.

With each new piece of evidence, it seemed more and more likely that these shootings were random. And if they were, who knew how long it would be until they caught this killer, or what motive the shooter had to begin with? If this was all just an assortment of random victims, the killer might be able to end a lot of other lives before being caught.

No, Charli wasn't going to accept that. The notion that there was no connection between any of the victims in the case made Charli's head spin. She was going to check that list herself and hope she'd be able to find something.

The issue wasn't that she didn't trust Brady or his team, of course. They were the FBI. Obviously, they knew what they were doing, but going over the list herself gave Charli some false sense of control, if only for a few minutes.

Once back in her office, she pulled up the list.

Matthew leaned down to read over her shoulder. "What are you doing?"

"I'm going to check again for any repeating names, and I'm going to make sure we checked the names of all the other victims. Maybe Pastor Layne was a patient. Or Roger Stanton. If they were, perhaps we have the connection we're looking for."

Neither Roger Stanton nor Victor Layne popped up on Gretta's list of patients, though. And after thoroughly cross-referencing each name on her patient list, Charli came up short. She let her head fall to her desk in an overdramatic gesture.

Matthew patted her shoulder. "I take it you didn't find anything."

Charli sat up, resting her cheek against her palm. "Not a thing."

It was difficult not to get discouraged by the many dead ends they'd encountered.

Matthew flashed her a sympathetic smile. "Don't get too down about it, Charli. We're going to find this guy. It's like you said. The more people he kills, the more information we get."

That may have been true, but how many more victims had to die before they found this madman?

21

Haley Reed glanced around at the circle of solemn faces before her. All ten of them were hollow, most of them atop thin, frail bodies, each in their own folding chair. The weight of the world was falling down on each set of bony shoulders, and it was Haley's job to somehow lift that weight, if only for an hour.

And even for that short period of time, the task seemed impossible.

"You have every right to feel however you need to feel, Dave. Just know that we're all here for you whenever those feelings seem overwhelming." Haley tucked her gray hair behind her ears. The waves were a little disheveled, and she could imagine the bags under her eyes were as dark as the eyes staring back at her.

But Haley made no effort to do her hair or wear makeup to these sessions. Not only would it be shallow to focus on her appearance while she spoke to the desperately ill, but looking her best also felt like bragging. Haley was a healthy weight, so she already stood in stark contrast with the gaunt bodies around her. She had no desire to flaunt her health to those who were losing theirs a little bit each day.

Dave only nodded in response. The room was silent, and Haley's gaze flitted from one person to the next. She never wanted to let the silence hang in the air too long, but she also struggled to put someone else on the spot if they didn't want to speak.

Haley's gaze landed on Emily. Blonde head tilted to the floor, the young woman rubbed her stained sneakers against each other, causing the rubber to squeak with the friction.

Only in her twenties, Emily was one of the youngest in the group and the person with the best prognosis. Though she'd been struggling with her cancer for two years, it was caught early, and Emily would likely go into remission.

Haley often called upon her when she felt the group could use a lighter conversation. And after Dave's confession that he often fantasized about suicide since learning he was terminal because it would allow him to have a modicum of control over his life, the group could definitely use a pick-me-up.

"What about you, Emily?" Haley's voice was gentle, like a heavy blanket wrapping around a chilled body.

Haley couldn't smile during these groups. It would come across as condescending when most of the faces surrounding her were filled with sorrow and tears. She was careful to make sure her voice was always inviting when her face could not be, though she tried to keep her expressions calming and empathetic rather than depressed.

Emily's body jolted up a bit, causing her shoes to squeak louder against the worn wood of the gymnasium floor. Her fingers clutched the jean jacket she was wearing closer to her chest, hiding away the white crop top underneath.

Emily's gaze met the floor once more. "What about me?"

This was more resistance than Haley usually got from Emily. "How is your week going?"

"Not great." Emily bit her glossed lip, refusing to make eye contact.

"We're here if you want to discuss it." This was an invitation Haley always provided when she sensed someone didn't care to talk. It left the door open in case they were just waiting to spill their feelings to someone while also giving them the option to withdraw.

There was a narrow tightrope that Haley had to walk as a grief counselor. The goal was never to push someone past their comfort zone, but a lot of people naturally became closed off when faced with uncomfortable topics, even if they were suffocated by their own silence. Haley had to encourage people without outright pushing them.

Emily finally lifted her head, exposing glistening green eyes. The quiver in her chin told Haley that this wasn't going to be the pick-me-up she had hoped for.

"I saw my doctor yesterday." Emily wiped a tear out of her right eye before it could fall to her cheek.

Haley's heartbeat quickened in her chest. "And how did that go?"

No matter how much she told herself she couldn't get attached to patients, she ached for every single one of them. It was impossible to talk to one another in this intimate setting without feeling connected. And their pain was her pain, whether she wanted it to be or not.

"He gave me six months. Six shitty months if I continue with the radiation. If I don't, it probably won't even be three." Saying it out loud was enough to puncture Emily's composure. She dropped her head into her hands, sobbing into her palms.

Haley swallowed hard, choking back her own tears. No, not sweet Emily. She was still just a kid. Not technically, of course. She was an adult in the eyes of the law, but nobody in their early twenties was truly an adult. The girl had barely lived.

How could this possibly be true? When the doctor had caught her melanoma, it had been at stage three. Emily had to go through surgery and treatment, but her at the time prognosis had been very good.

Apparently, not anymore.

Emily lifted her head, tears still streaming down her face. "I don't know what to do. I thought when this was all done, I'd get to go to college, but that's never going to happen now. I'll never have a husband or kids. My life is over."

Shaken to her core, Haley couldn't think of a word to say as she fought against the emotion trying to overwhelm her. During times like these, Haley questioned the validity of her job. There were no words of comfort when someone was facing death's door. Emily wasn't going to get any silver linings. How would this group actually bring her any solace?

But Haley had to remember that, above all else, Emily needed to talk. Whether they had fifty years left or just a few hours, everyone needed to be able to speak about their emotions and life experiences. Emily likely didn't have anyone to talk to about her feelings. Many people with terminal illnesses didn't want to burden family and friends, knowing that they were experiencing their own grief. That was what this group was here for.

"I'm so deeply sorry, Emily. I cannot imagine what you must be feeling right now." Haley scanned each face and found that Emily's eyes were not the only ones filled with tears.

"Yeah. I can't really imagine it either." Emily's sobs had eased up a bit, though her breaths were still punctuated by long pauses.

In other types of counseling, it was common to come up

with a plan of action for a patient to help improve their life, but there was no adequate therapeutic intervention for someone's life ending.

Out in the real world, Haley had seen people react to the terminally ill in the most unhelpful ways. They'd say, "You never know when a cure might pop up," completely oblivious to the fact that, even if a cure came out tomorrow, it would likely be too late for those whose bodies had been ravaged by their cancer. Or they'd say, "You have to live every moment to the fullest," as if these people didn't already treasure every breath they had left.

In the group, Haley's patients were safe from useless platitudes that did nothing to help their situation.

Haley put her hands on her lap. "And you don't have to sort your feelings out all at once. If you're sad, you are entitled to those feelings. Be angry. Be bitter. You have no obligation to anyone to rein in your emotions right now. Just focus on you."

That was all Emily could do now. Seeming to understand that fact, the young woman nodded in silence but didn't seem to want to say more. Haley made a mental note to check on her individually at the end of the group session. She always prioritized talking to her patients who had recently received devastating news. Haley also needed to make sure she referred Emily to the group that was specifically for the terminally ill.

While this current group had many terminally ill patients, the group was open to anyone struggling with a life-threatening diagnosis. Haley ran several different groups out of the high school gymnasium three evenings a week. It was part of a publicly funded initiative by Savannah to provide free grief counseling.

Haley not only worked with those who were sick, but she also held grief groups for those who had recently experi-

enced the death of a loved one. She was one of many certi-
fied counselors working with the city.

Although Emily was silent for the remainder of the
group, her tear-streaked cheeks didn't escape Haley's notice
for a second. Every once in a while, Emily reached out to
swipe at a stray tear coursing down her face. Haley cared
deeply for each and every person she counseled, but because
Emily was so young and vulnerable, there was a special kind
of ache in Haley's heart tonight. A young woman like her did
not deserve to have her life cut short.

When the session ended, Emily rushed out of there quick
as lightning. Although Haley tried to follow her outside, the
young woman was on her bike and down the road before
Haley could ask her to come back.

She could have called out, but that wasn't an appropriate
move. Emily was sending clear signals she had no desire to
speak to anyone, and Haley had to honor that.

When everyone had left the gymnasium, Haley allowed
herself a few tears as she emptied out the coffee pot and
folded the donut boxes she'd brought in. She was always
telling everyone else to feel their emotions. Haley couldn't
stop from feeling her own for a least a few moments.

"I'm so sorry, Emily." The whispered words meant
nothing.

Crushed by the gravity of each person's story, Haley knelt
in the middle of the gym and did something she rarely did.
She prayed.

Not just for Emily, though seeing a woman in her twenties losing her life was certainly cause to beg any higher
power for mercy. There were so many others in pain who
deserved healing. People with kids they'd never see get
married. Those who had just lost their spouse, who was the
breadwinner. The string of heartbreak was infinite. No

matter how many people Haley tried to help, there were always more whose lives were being torn apart.

With a soft, "Amen," Haylee pushed to her feet and straightened her shoulders. She'd felt her feelings, had her little breakdown. Now, she had to pull herself together so she could do it all over again tomorrow.

Haley had decided to bear the burden of others for one simple reason...she knew she could. She was strong. If she could help just one person, everything was worth it.

And she had time to focus on those who entrusted their personal stories to her. When Haley went home tonight, she would enter an empty one-bedroom apartment. She didn't have so much as a cat to keep her company. Never married, she hadn't been close to her family for years. Haley's only human connection was through her work, and she was okay with that. More than okay. Actually, she was proud of it.

When heavy footfalls moved into the gymnasium, she didn't turn around right away. Having a member return after a group session wasn't unusual, and she specifically kept the gymnasium doors open while cleaning up in case someone came in to speak with her in confidence. She folded in the pink donut box so it wouldn't spill, and with a gentle smile, she turned around.

To Haley's surprise, it wasn't anyone from the group session tonight, but that was no problem. She recognized him as someone who'd been a part of her group sessions before.

"It's been a while." Haley's cheery voice echoed in the now empty gymnasium. "Care for a donut?"

"You think I'm here for donuts?"

The monotone voice caused the smile to slide from her face, and she took a step back. Although the newcomer was at least ten feet away, she had the urge to distance herself from him further.

Something was terribly wrong. With an instinct she didn't realize she possessed, Haley knew this wasn't a friendly visit. Had this cold, dead look been in his eyes when he'd been part of her sessions before?

No. She would have remembered if that had been the case. She'd never before witnessed eyes that were so dead yet burning with rage at the same time.

What was his name? Mark? Mike? He'd always been so quiet and unassuming that her brain refused to serve up the correct identification.

A bubble of nausea formed in Haley's stomach. She'd been trained extensively on how to handle people's grief and the anger that came with it. There was no question she knew how to de-escalate certain situations. But a little voice in her head told her this was not the kind of anger that accompanied grief. Whatever this was, she had no technique to calm it.

So, she needed to stay calm herself.

Haley took a deep breath, wiping her clammy palms on the sides of her pants. "What can I do for you?"

He smiled, but instead of the gesture being reassuring, it only increased her terror. The look on the man's face reminded Haley of the cartoon villains she had watched as a kid.

"You look bothered." He took a slow, deliberate step toward Haley. "I want you to know it's okay to feel all your feelings."

Haley swallowed hard. *What is he talking about?* "Excuse me?"

"You heard me. Isn't that what you're always saying? Just feel your feelings? As if that's somehow going to help?" His face was blank, his tone even. The man was so unnerving that Haley wished he would just scream the words. Anything would be better than this chilling calm.

She glanced at the door behind him. *There's no way I can make it outside before he tackles me to the ground.*

"Yes, I do say that." Haley straightened her spine, willing herself to exude a confidence she didn't feel. But what was the use? All the confidence in the world wouldn't be able to keep her safe from this deranged man.

He walked in a circle around her, the squeak of shoes against the gym floor now quiet as he stopped somewhere behind her. "You've never faced your own mortality, have you, Haley?"

Haley spun around to face the man, but he resumed his path around her, so she had to pivot to continue to face him. She glanced around, but she found nothing she could use as a weapon except the half-empty box of donuts.

Why did I leave my purse in the locker room? If I had my cell phone, I could call 9-1-1.

"No, I haven't."

"Then who the hell are you to tell people how to deal with their impending death, huh?" He continued to circle around her like a lion stalking its prey. Like the animal he was imitating, his voice was a low growl. "You ever lost anyone, Haley? Ever had someone close to you die?"

Admittedly, Haley hadn't. She only had a few friends and no family to speak of. And even most of her estranged family was alive and well.

"No, I haven't." Haley's hands trembled, and it was a concerted effort to keep her voice steady.

Why did this man hold such animosity toward her? What had she done?

"Please tell me what I've done to harm you, and I'll do my best to make it right."

Though her mind was hijacked by fear, she still attempted to scroll through her memory, tried to remember any argument or fight from when he'd attended sessions. In fact, if memory served, hadn't she'd helped him? What was his problem, coming in here in a rage?

"Make it right?" His laugh was like nails clawing down the chalkboard of her composure. "Do you even have a clue as to what that might be? Do you?" He stopped pacing and faced her. "I tell you what…tell me how you've wronged me, and I won't be forced to use this."

Reaching into his jacket pocket, she nearly fainted when he pulled out a gun.

Sweet Lord, please have mercy.

But even as she thought the prayer, Haylee knew this man had no mercy to give. Giving herself a mental shake, she forced herself to fall back on her training.

Focus. You have to keep him talking.

"I m-must have said something terrible to you. I-I'm s-so s-sorry."

Hollow laughter rang out as he aimed the gun at her chest. "Man, you really are a shitty therapist."

Holding out both hands as if they could stop a bullet, bile rose in her throat. She swallowed it down. "I'm incredibly sorry for hurting you. Please tell me what you need me to do to help you, and we can work through this together. I can understand why you'd have a lot of rage right now and—"

"You don't, though." He strode toward her, closing the distance between them, the gun still aimed straight at her chest. "Do you? That's the problem. You don't understand. You couldn't understand unless you were looking death in the face." He took one more step and jammed the gun against her temple. "So, congratulations, Haley. You're now looking death in the face. If you've ever understood me, it's right here. Right now."

Hot tears welled in Haley's eyes before burning a trail down her cheeks. "Please, I don't want to—"

"Die?!" His voice boomed, echoing off the gym walls.

"Nobody ever does! Tell me, does it help if I tell you to feel your feelings?"

"No." She croaked out the reply as tears streamed down her face. "Please…"

She squeezed her eyes shut, but the darkness behind her eyelids was no reprieve from the nightmare she was living.

"Do you really want to know what you did to me?"

As the steel of the barrel moved away from her skin, Haley's eyes flew open. "Y-yes."

He lowered the gun and stepped away. "It's the worst thing one human being can do to another."

Breathing out a shaky breath, Haley thought she might have a chance of surviving this encounter. She strengthened her voice. "Please tell me."

The gun centered on her chest again. "You gave me hope."

A flash of fire was the last thing she ever saw.

22

As Haley Reed's body dropped to the floor, blood splattered across the glistening wood. Would they be able to get the blood cleaned off before the kids returned to school? Did I care?

Yes.

For the span of a heartbeat, a pang of guilt penetrated my chest. The emotion took me by surprise.

Why should I feel guilty? Wasn't I ridding the planet of one more useless, sniveling piece of trash? A liar? A breaker of promises and destroyer of faith?

"That bitch deserved to die. Time to go."

Damian was right...on both counts.

As fast as it had come, the guilt faded, strengthening my resolve. I needed to get out of here. I couldn't get caught... not yet. I had two more tokens in my pocket that needed to be delivered.

Pulling the ski mask back down over my face, I glanced one last time at Haley. It was a mistake because my mind flashed to other times we'd been together in this very room. I could see her standing in front of my little group. Watching her face as my fellow support group members cried over the loss of their own future.

There was a time when I actually thought she was kind. That she might be helping me process my diagnosis.

"Feel your feelings."

"Don't lose hope."

"Miracles happen every day. That miracle could be you."

When I was told that I was terminal, I realized a simple truth...my feelings and faith didn't matter, and that hope was a brutal bitch that would knife you in the heart.

Now, no other participant would sit in a chair and listen to those vile promises.

So, I had no other choice than to kill her, right? This wasn't just for me. I had to shoot that smug little bitch for everyone who had to deal with her condescending ramblings. Hell, I wasn't even sure she actually cared about these people. This was her job. The state paid her to be here, and state jobs came with good benefits. When a hefty paycheck was involved, could I trust that her advice was even real?

"Penny for your thoughts."

That was another line Haley had used to coax us to talk. To *feel our feelings.*

Pulling a token from my pocket, I tossed it at her face. "Here you go." Now, I was paid in full.

"You're wasting time."

Damian punctuated his words with a knife twist in my gut that very nearly sent me to my knees. Long seconds ticked by before his grip on my insides released.

Breathing hard and sweating profusely, I staggered for the door.

Yes. *Time's a-wastin'!*

I was nearly home when my phone began to ring. That nagging bitch had better not be calling me to ask me where I was. How many times did I have to tell her to leave me the hell alone? That I would be home when I was home? I was sick of having to check in like I was a teenager with a curfew.

But it wasn't my wife calling. It was my boss.

No doubt, he'd been wondering about my whereabouts for the past week. I hadn't called in to work. Not that I had to. My job was remote, so nobody would ever know if I played hooky for a day.

But I hadn't just played hooky for a day or even two or three. I hadn't worked for a couple weeks now. My emails were piling up, and I wasn't answering. For the old me, that was out of character. The old me was a diligent employee, always going the extra mile.

Before I met Damian, I finished writing my technical manuscripts a week before they were due. Had those assholes ever given me a bonus for the hard work I'd put in for the company?

Hell no.

To think that I once attained a great deal of satisfaction from trying to please these people made me sick.

What a beta move.

Never again.

I wasn't going to waste my time on them anymore. There was a pile of overdue tasks waiting for me, but they were never going to get done. Hadn't I given this company enough of my life? They didn't deserve any more.

"Kill him too."

Damian's thirst for blood made me smile. "Maybe I will, but he's not a high priority right now."

"Think of the misery he's caused you over the years. He deserves to die."

Damian wasn't wrong.

Pulling into my driveway, I let the Honda CRV idle. My wife's old Accord was hidden where no one would find it. I doubted I'd need that heap of junk anymore. Everything from this point would be nice and personal.

When the porch light turned on, I realized I'd been sitting in the driveway for nearly a half hour. Where had the time gone? And why, with so little of it left, was I sitting out here all alone?

Because of her.

No part of me wanted to go inside and see my wife. She was just another thing I'd wasted a life on. There was no passion in our relationship, and I tried to remember a day when there had been. We'd barely had sex a handful of times in the last few years. Now, I was about to croak, never having ravaged a woman the way I was meant to. The way I deserved to.

"Do it."

I snorted at Damian's suggestion. With my diagnosis, I was no longer able to get it up. Yet another personal attack on my body and mind.

"Maybe you just need to find the right woman."

Flashy long nails popped into my mind, and I could almost imagine the good doctor's receptionist digging them into my skin as I slid my cock in and out of her inflated lips.

What the hell?

I must truly be going crazy if that plastic Barbie of a receptionist was the first woman to pop into my mind.

It wasn't fair.

Someone so vain shouldn't have the right to continue breathing.

When it came down to it, I knew I was right to rid our planet of the people on my list to correct the unfairness that had been heaped against me.

The world was only fair if I made it fair.

23

M atthew scanned the area as Charli parked a block away from the horde of flashing red and blue lights. "Man, this is a lot of cop cars."

Although Matthew and Charli were only a few miles away when they'd heard the police chatter on the radio about shots fired, Special Agent Jay Brady and his men were already on the scene at the corner of East Avenue and 52nd.

But had there actually been gunshots, or had someone heard a loud noise and called 9-1-1? The entire city was now on high alert, ready to jump at the slightest hint of a threat. When a killer had every citizen up in arms about a serial murderer, even a firework going off would set off a panic.

Which was exactly why Matthew was suspicious there had been true gunfire. The high school sat on that corner, and it seemed much more likely it was some students messing around after hours.

When they pulled up, roadblocks were already being set out around the perimeter of the school. On any other case, Matthew would've considered this reaction to be overkill, but he couldn't blame Brady for being cautious.

Brady waved them down as Matthew and Charli signed themselves into the logbook. He seemed to be directing every responder on the scene.

"Detective Cross, Detective Church." His robotic expression didn't move as he turned to them. "Glad you're here. We haven't found a shooting victim yet, but SWAT's on their way and the plan is to clear every building on the school property. I'm sending arriving teams to canvass the block to see what they can find."

Perhaps this was because there wasn't a victim to find. "And where do you want us?"

"I need you two walking the school grounds. That's our next priority. Put your gear on and keep me informed. And make sure you don't enter any buildings until SWAT has cleared them. I'll keep you updated." Brady tapped the screen of his iPad, indicating a map of the school campus he'd already pulled up. "You two head north on this side. Radio when you've cleared the external area."

Charli nodded. "We're on it."

Although Matthew had complained to Charli in the past about the FBI and GBI taking over their cases, he knew better than to argue. Besides, with shootings happening all over the city, they could use the extra manpower. As much as he loved to work on a case when it was just him and Charli, the killer was escalating, and he was grateful for the help.

Plus, truth be told, Brady seemed very capable and quick on his feet. Matthew appreciated those two traits. Even if the man had a cyborg brain.

Matthew wondered if Charli was as dubious as he was. "Think we'll find anything?"

Charli shrugged. "Maybe. Or maybe we'll rule out a gunshot and let the neighborhood get some sleep."

She was right.

If they searched the grounds of the high school, they

might find out the source of the noise. If they found evidence of fireworks having been shot recently, they'd be able to return their attention to the previous shootings.

Matthew got his flashlight out, pointing it ahead of them. There was still a twinge of pain in his right forearm from the knife wound, but it had healed enough to be only a minor nuisance. "Maybe this isn't our guy, but just some random noise."

Charli only pressed her lips together, which meant she wasn't ready to provide a theory just yet.

The school wasn't a single structure but a series of different buildings with classroom doors that led outside, so the campus had many entrances. That made it easy for kids to return to school and cause a ruckus or spray-paint classroom doors. Back in his years as a beat cop, Matthew had been dispatched to the school often.

"Yeah? Why do you think that?" Charli fished out her own flashlight. The deeper they moved into the school grounds, the darker it became as they left the streetlights behind.

"Like Brady said, our killer has worked exclusively in drive-bys. And if he shot someone on this street, we would've been able to easily find them by now. If this is the same man, I don't think he rushed into a nearby house to kill someone on private property."

He didn't have to remind Charli of Savannah's crime rate outside of their current case. The sound some bystander heard could have many sources, from the fireworks he favored to domestic violence down the street.

Charli scanned her flashlight over the tennis courts as they passed. "I don't know. We still don't know this man's motive. He's killed a lot of people in a short span of time, which means we only have insight into what he's been thinking for the past few days."

"So, you think these past few days, our killer wanted to go

for a drive, but tonight he decided on a change of scenery?" Matthew didn't attempt to stop a sarcastic chuckle. "I don't know, Charli. I think he's made his preferred style of murder clear."

Charli stopped, training her flashlight beam on a squatty looking bush, walking around it to thoroughly examine the area. "You could be right. There's also the possibility that, even if the noise was a gunshot, it's unrelated to the recent shootings. This is Savannah, after all."

Although Matthew was doubtful their killer had come through this area on foot, there was something eerie about the empty school grounds. Around any one of these buildings, someone could be lurking, biding their time until their next victim turned the corner.

As they walked, Matthew held the flashlight with one hand and rested the other hand on his gun holster. His skepticism was never going to keep him from being prepared, and he kept their conversation to a minimum so that their presence wouldn't be announced if there actually was someone lying in wait nearby.

After making their way halfway around the school without incident, Matthew caught a glimpse of light shining from the gym windows.

Charli had seen it too. "Are those lights always on?"

He had no idea.

"Not sure how they do things now, but when I was in school, I remember them flipping off the lights after everyone left the basketball games."

Charli let out a short gasp as she raised her hand to her chest. "Wait, are you telling me they had electricity in the Stone Age?"

Matthew rolled his eyes, but he doubted Charli saw him in the darkness. "By my teen years, Benjamin Franklin had it figured out. But sure, it was pretty dark in elementary school."

Charli swatted him on the shoulder. "Come on. Let's circle the perimeter."

As they crept along side by side, Matthew scanned every bush and tree with his flashlight. With every measured step, a twinge of anxiety rolled through him. No matter how positive he'd been that, when they reached the front of the gymnasium, they'd find the doors locked and the building empty, he'd started to have a funny feeling in his gut that maybe his first instinct had been wishful thinking.

He shoved the nagging in his gut aside. The most likely scenario was that someone had simply forgotten to turn off the lights at the end of basketball practice. But when they turned the front corner of the building, they were greeted by a wide-open door.

Why would it be unlocked and open? Especially since the gymnasium parking lot was empty.

Had SWAT or another team already arrived? He pulled up a mental image of Special Agent Brady's iPad and remembered specifically that the agent hadn't yet assigned this area to anyone else.

Charli turned to Matthew, motioning him forward with her flashlight. The light emanating from it illuminated her face, adding a wave of shadows that had Matthew even more on edge.

Matthew held up a hand. "No way, Charli. I doubt this building's been cleared yet. Brady will have our heads if we go in there now."

Charli put a hand on her hip. "Come on, Matt. Just a quick peek to find out why the light's on. We'll just glance around and step right back out."

Matthew groaned low in his throat. Why did his partner

have to be so stubborn? Sometimes, he swore Charli had been a mule in another life.

As they prepared to enter the building, Matthew drew his weapon and moved to Charli's side. He might doubt the notion that there was anyone inside, but he wasn't foolish enough to take any chances.

Lup-dup. Lup-dup. Lup-dup.

Matthew's heart sped up, the damn thing threatening to pound out of his chest. He drew in a steady breath, forcing his breathing to slow.

Did his heart know something his gut hadn't figured out yet?

What the hell were they about to find? Something horrible or two teens going at it behind the bleachers? Had a crime occurred or were they about to walk into an empty building in which someone had forgotten to turn off the lights after basketball practice?

He simply didn't know, especially since his heart and gut seemed to be in disagreement. One thing he did know, though, was this...whoever had killed three people and set the entire city on edge was batshit crazy. And as much as they'd tried to predict the murderer's next move, they were only grasping at straws.

Charli held up three fingers on her hand.

Then moved one down, leaving two.

She moved one more to her palm.

Then finally, the last finger went down, and they turned the corner together.

The sight sucker punched Matthew in the gut.

There was no need for them to go any farther. The bleachers were folded up into the wall, so the entire gymnasium was visible. Next to a folding table in the middle of the gym, a female victim was sprawled on the floor. Blood circled her body, seeping into her light gray hair.

As Matthew kept his gun trained on the corners of the gym, Charli crept closer to the victim, avoiding the pools of blood. Even as she knelt and placed her fingertips to the woman's neck, he knew their victim was dead.

A moment later, Charli shook her head and pulled out her cell. "Agent Brady, I have some very bad news."

24

Charli's head was still spinning as Preston Powell relayed the news that they'd found the victim's purse in the women's locker room.

The woman they'd found dead in a pool of her own blood was fifty-one-year-old Haley Reed. She had a master's in social work, and according to the Department of Social Services of Savannah, she ran multiple grief counseling groups out of the high school gymnasium as well as a local community center.

"Why Haley Reed?" Charli glanced between Preston and Matthew. "And is this a random crime or could it be connected in any way to our current shooting spree?"

That was the million-dollar question.

Matthew tossed up his hands. "How could it be connected? Our other three vics were shot in a quick and convenient drive-by. Now, he entered a high school gymnasium at night to kill his next victim?"

Matt was right. This didn't add up.

But still…something was telling Charli to not render her opinion so quickly.

"Let's say that our shooter is the doer in this case as well." She held up a hand when Matthew opened his mouth to argue. "Because we've not been able to discover any connection between the victims, I've been leaning toward our current murder spree being random and the victims chosen out of convenience."

Preston rubbed his chin, listening closely. "Go on."

"But…and I know this is a big but, what if Haley Reed was targeted by our same perp." She waved a hand toward the body still on the gym floor. "There's nothing convenient about going into a high school after hours to find someone to shoot, not when it would be so easy to drive around town and kill someone walking along the sidewalk."

"Charli, I know you don't like to get tunnel vision. I don't either. But what you're suggesting is a stretch." Matthew folded his arms in front of him. "First, the shooter would've had to know this group existed, which is odd because I didn't even know this group existed before tonight. And it seems like a damn useful resource provided by the city. Why kill a woman doing good?"

Matthew was right. But still…

Preston glanced at Matthew before focusing his gaze on Charli. "If what you're thinking is true, either he knew about the group, or he knew about Haley. Could just be he was aware of her job, and he had it out for her."

Charli blinked, surprised the GBI agent hadn't shot her growing theory down.

Pivoting around to avoid Preston's penetrating gaze, Charli turned to face the rest of the gym. It was swarming with people now. As agents ran around at Jay Brady's instruction, Soames and his forensic team scurried around taking photos and collecting evidence. One of the team picked up the pink donut box with gloved hands, checking for possible fingerprints.

Although the scene was chaotic, chaos was where Charli thrived. This was why she was so good in this line of work. She drew in a deep breath before turning back to face Preston and Matthew.

"Before we're directed to call Haley Reed's murder an isolated incident, I want to look for a connection between her and the other victims. If we can—"

"I need someone to check the perimeter of this building and all buildings around the student parking lot to check for cameras." Brady's booming voice startled Charli, his words commanding the attention of every person in the room. "I want to know if a Honda was in the lot. We need to either confirm or rule out that this murder was conducted by the same person. And the sooner we can do that, the better. It's going to take time for ballistics to get us an answer."

Charli couldn't help but remember Matthew's comment about Brady being robotic. No matter how tense the situation became, the agent's voice stayed calm yet decisive. She admired the man and could see why he'd made it to the FBI when he was so controlled under pressure.

Jumping at the chance to escape the crowded gym, Charli headed for the door. "I'll do it, sir." She could use the quiet time to run through their options.

Preston Powell's voice rang out behind her. "I'll assist."

Charli resisted the urge to roll her eyes. So much for a silent moment to mull over the case.

Preston's footsteps matched Charli's as they headed outside. They were only a few steps down the sidewalk before he caught her arm. "I can't help but feel like you're avoiding me."

I'm so not wanting to have this conversation right now.

She sidestepped the question and began walking again, glad when he didn't attempt to contain her. "We're working together. How could I avoid you?"

Preston shoved his hands in his pockets as he caught up with her. "Well, you're obviously not avoiding me at work. But after our time together, I thought, you know, you might give me a call."

The cool night breeze blew Charli's short hair away from her face. "I don't know if that's entirely fair. You didn't call me either." She turned on her flashlight and pointed it at the brick wall of the building, scanning the edges of the roof.

Was Preston even looking for a security camera? His focus seemed to be only on her. "Well, I didn't think you wanted me to call. Are you saying you did?"

Charli fought not to growl. How was she supposed to focus on the case at hand when all Preston wanted to do was discuss their relationship? If she could even call it that. She didn't exactly consider one hurried night together after an exhausting day at work and one too many drinks a relationship.

Irritation crawled over her skin.

As much as Charli itched to set him straight, it wouldn't help the situation. Deep down, she knew that Preston was a good guy and an excellent GBI agent. Hell, they'd even shared a few brief moments of chemistry, and before their less than stellar night together had made things awkward between them, Charli had actually considered him as a person she could date. Not anymore.

Keep telling yourself that.

Pissed at her inner voice's contradiction, she knew that she might very well be having a classic "the lady doth protest too much" moment. Okay, fine.

Maybe she did find him attractive. And sure, maybe she was using their tepid night together as an excuse to paint him in a bad light. But right now, with her plate as full as it was, she simply didn't want to be in a relationship.

No. You just don't want to be hurt.

The truth of the words were like a slap, which pissed her off even more. This was why she didn't do relationships. This right here. They were only a distraction from what she needed to be doing.

If Charli didn't nip this in the bud right now, Preston was going to distract her even more, and she wouldn't let one bad decision to sleep with him impact her job.

Armoring herself, Charli lifted her chin. "Look, Preston, I think you're a great guy, but when I decided to, you know, go out with you, I didn't realize we'd be working together again, at least not so soon. As a rule, I don't date colleagues. There is...was an attraction between us, and maybe there's still something there, but for the time being, I have too much going on in my life to entertain the thought of a relationship right now, even a casual one." She flashed him a weak smile. "I like you and respect you, and I think you're a phenomenal agent, but I'd really just like to be friends."

Even in the dim light, it was easy for Charli to make out the fading smile on Preston's face, and she remembered why she'd found him so handsome in the first place. But he was a gentleman and a professional, so he didn't complain.

He gave a calm, solemn nod. "Thank you for your honesty. I can respect that, but I do want you to know that, just because we've tabled this discussion for now, that doesn't mean I won't ask you out again in the future."

She didn't attempt to contain a soft smile. "Fair enough. But for now, let's just focus on finding our killer." She reached out and touched his arm for a brief second, surprising herself. "I'm glad you're on this case with me."

She meant every word.

Silence became a living thing between them for the space of a few heartbeats, and Charli resisted the urge to step closer to him. He must have felt the tug too because he shifted his focus away from her and scanned the outer walls of the brick building, though there wasn't much to see.

Shaking their conversation and the feelings it had stirred in her off, Charli moved her flashlight from one side of the building to the other as she scanned it but fell short of finding anything. "We can keep looking at the other buildings. There's bound to be a camera somewhere."

Preston sighed and nodded. "Yeah, you'd think so. You'd be shocked by the kind of crimes I've seen at local schools. A lot of drug deals going down on school grounds."

"These days, I believe it." Even when Charli had been in school nearly ten years ago, she'd witnessed some sketchy things. "Dammit, though. I was really hoping we could get a solid lead on our killer. Right now, we don't even know if this is the same person."

Preston ran a hand through his hair. "We can still act as though it is the same killer. If it isn't, then time will tell that. But if we wait for confirmation to continue our investigation, we're just giving this psycho more time to continue his killing spree. Whoever they are, they've shown no desire to slow down. At this rate, I wouldn't be surprised if there was another murder by morning."

Charli could only imagine how stressed Ruth must be right now. This was the one scenario she feared. At this rate, this killer was going to outdo the Beltway sniper attacks.

Preston's phone rang, and he leaned against the brick building as he picked up. "Agent Powell here. Uh-huh. Got it. Okay, thank you." Preston turned to face Charli. "Just got the background on Haley Reed. No husband, no kids, only family member is her mother in a retirement home, apparently with dementia, so she's an unreliable source. No prior arrests or any criminal history to speak of."

Charli rolled her head, stretching the muscles in her neck

and shoulders. "So, we've got nobody who knows her who would have any insight into why someone might harm her. What about people she worked with or her clients?"

"We're working on that. Right now, we're checking her socials. Maybe someone has made threats to her online." But it was obvious that Preston was grasping at straws as much as she was.

And Charli doubted that. Most of the time, when someone made public threats of homicide, it didn't amount to much. People who were impulsive enough to make threats in a fit of rage rarely had the wherewithal to go through with the threats. Most killers moved in silence, and this murderer was clearly calculated. He'd left so little information for them to go off of.

Charli massaged her temples in slow circles. "We're the ones who are going to have to find this connection."

As if right on cue, Matthew jogged up. "Charli! We found this on the floor near the folding table." He had his phone in his gloved hand, waving it in the air.

Charli raised her eyebrows. "You found your own phone?"

He grinned, shaking his head from side to side. "No! Of course not. I just snapped a photo." Matthew stopped when he was in between Powell and Charli. "It's the sign-in sheets from her grief sessions today."

Finally, we have something we can work with.

This was exactly the link Charli needed. If Haley Reed was as much of a hermit as her initial background check made it appear, then they'd have to look into her professional life for connections to the other victims.

"This won't be enough, though." Charli turned toward Preston. "Did the Department of Social Services say whether these were Haley Reed's only support group sessions?"

"They didn't." Matthew sucked in a breath and leaned

down, resting his hands on his knees. "But since these grief groups are only three days a week, I doubt it. She likely does therapy sessions at other locations."

Charli patted him on the back. *How many times do I have to beg you to go for a run with me? If you'd start exercising again, you wouldn't be sucking down air like you haven't breathed in a week.*

"We've got to run all these names against the other lists we have, but I need lists of all her group participants. And I want to know if the city is holding grief group sessions anywhere else."

Both Preston and Matthew gave Charli a puzzled glance, their exhaustion no doubt slowing down their mental faculties, but Matthew spoke first. "Why do we need to know other grief group locations?"

Come on, Matt. Isn't it obvious?

"Look, we don't know if Haley Reed was actually a target tonight or if it was the grief group in general that was the target of our killer. This is a severely demented person we're dealing with. For all we know, they could be targeting grief groups simply because they're sadistic enough to cause grieving people to suffer further. We need to cover all the bases."

Although Charli was leaning toward these murders not being random, she couldn't rule it out. The only thing they could eliminate was the fact that this particular murder wasn't one made out of convenience. This one had been deliberate. But for now, that was all they knew.

Preston raised his fist at Charli, and she bumped him back. "Charli, you're truly a genius. I'll go speak to Brady. I'll be in touch and get you those lists as soon as possible. And then we can..."

Preston lifted his hand to his face to block out the blinding headlights from a vehicle.

Charli squinted as she studied who had driven onto the

campus, but even in the glare, she knew. It was a news van with two more behind it.

Oh, boy. Ruth was going to love this.

25

C harli groaned and slammed her palm on the dash. She'd hoped and prayed that when they got back to the precinct, they'd be able to escape the bright lights of news vans.

Of course not.

They were dotted all over the parking lot, like a swarm of bees ready to sting. Even worse, the back entrance was also flooded with reporters.

"I've never seen anything like this." Charli cut the steering wheel to the right to pull into a space. "And here I thought the Mowery case was bad with the press. This is just completely over the top. We're not going to make it to the building without being harassed."

Matthew clicked the buckle to release his seat belt. "This isn't the Mowery case, Charli. It's so much worse. Sure, people are interested when a rich person gets arrested. It's juicy. News vans will show up for that. But it's not nearly as big of a story as the entire town being terrorized by one man."

It hit Charli all at once that this was one of the biggest

cases they'd ever handled. Sure, they'd had serial murderers before. They'd had cases where the FBI was brought in. But even in those cases, the killers were behaving in a slow and deliberate manner, like the killer who'd stalked, captured, and tortured teen girls before gruesomely dismembering them.

Maybe this wasn't as gruesome, but it was far scarier to the average citizen of Savannah. With that case, people could reassure themselves that if they weren't a teen girl, they were safe. And even if they were, or they had a teen daughter, they'd be able to keep her safe by not allowing her to roam the city alone because the serial killer had to snatch someone up in order to kill them.

But this case? People were being shot on the streets. None of these victims could have prevented what happened to them. These poor people never saw their deaths coming, and they didn't have to suffer for long once the killer targeted them.

The only way to stay safe was not to leave the house, but that simply wasn't possible for most citizens of Savannah. They had to go to work, run errands, go to school, and they couldn't just put their lives on hold. And even if they did venture out, and the press jumped the gun and tried to connect Haley Reed's murder to the drive-bys, residents might not even feel safe in their homes anymore.

Whoever this killer was, they had managed to force the entire city to live in fear. Was that the point? Perhaps the victims were not the direct targets of the killer but simply part of a grand design to instill fear in Savannah.

If that was the goal, the killer was doing an amazing job, and it rocked Charli to the core how easily they'd been able to pull it off. A single person could bring a community to its knees with just a few bullets.

But what if there was more than one killer working

together? Even worse, what if the shootings weren't even related? Although Charli wanted to believe all the cases were connected, they didn't have the evidence to prove it.

Charli took in a deep, calming breath. "What are we going to say to them? They're going to drown us in questions."

Matthew put a hand on her shoulder. "We say the only thing we can, that we're not at liberty to discuss the case. Because we're not, and nothing we say is going to comfort people right now. They want answers we do not have." Though Matthew was stating a fact, there was a softness in his voice that provided Charli a small measure of comfort.

Charli unbuckled her seat belt. "All right. Let's get out and face the music."

A handful of reporters swarmed Charli and Matthew as they moved to the back exit. Since she didn't make eye contact with any of them, Charli didn't know who asked which question. She barely even registered their physical appearance as she kept her gaze on the path to the door.

"Are you two detectives on the case?"

"What do you know about this murderer?"

"Was the latest victim killed by the same shooter?"

"Are people safe in their own homes anymore?"

The frenzied questions rang out, and the way the reporters were all shouting over each other, Charli wasn't even sure how they expected to hear her answer.

Just outside the door, Charli turned to give them their soundbite. She lifted a hand for quiet. "We are not at liberty to discuss details of the case at this time, but we're working diligently to keep the citizens of Savannah safe."

On her last word, Matthew opened the back door for her, and she scurried inside. The press was still shouting questions over each other as the door slammed in their faces.

Charli threw her hands into the air. "What the hell? Do they think this is going to help us do our jobs?"

Matthew's jaw was clenched. "I don't think they care. They just want the latest scoop so people will tune into their morning broadcasts. They're worse than vultures, I swear. Maybe if they didn't play into the terror, our shooter wouldn't be able to cause the public at large so much distress."

They were silent as they made their way to their office. When they approached the open door, Sergeant Ruth Morris was already waiting, sitting in Charli's chair with her tell-me-you-have-a-lead look on her face.

"Did you two manage to avoid the press on your way in?"

Charli took off her jacket. The stress of walking by reporters and realizing the gravity of their case was dampening her armpits. "Are you kidding me? They're at every part of the building. But we only provided the standard 'we're not at liberty' statement."

"Good." Ruth rubbed her hand along the back of her neck. Charli could tell the stress was getting to her too. It was getting to everyone. "Last I heard, we were trying to get a list of Haley Reed's clients and the locations of other city-sanctioned grief counseling locations. Have we done that?"

"Agent Powell is still working on it." Charli leaned against her desk. "But as much as I want to believe there is only one shooter and each of these murders are related, I feel like we're still at square one. And we have no idea what this psycho or psychos might be planning."

Ruth closed her eyes and squeezed the bridge of her nose while Matthew tapped his pen in succession against the top of his desk.

Charli strolled over to the murder board, taking in each victim's name. "Let's look at the kind of people that are being killed here. A minister, an x-ray tech, a mini-mart owner, and a grief counselor. Assuming we have just one shooter, could it be that our killer had someone close to him die?

Perhaps they're out to punish people they believe didn't do enough to help."

Ruth rose from Charli's chair. "If that's what you think, get me a name. A name on any of our lists that matches up. You both know I want that more than anything. I don't want this to be random. But until we know more, we follow Brady's lead."

The office was quiet after Ruth shut the door behind her. Charli examined the victims' faces one more time before heading to her desk. "I'm going to get that name. I don't care if I have to wait here all night. I'm getting that name."

Charli didn't typically go with gut instincts, but this wasn't a feeling. It was a logical connection...at least in her head. While it may not initially appear that their victims had much in common, all these career fields could be involved with someone who was dying.

And a dead loved one could easily send someone who was already mentally unwell down a dark road. This wouldn't be the first time that a killer set out for vengeance after a person they cared about passed away.

Charli still wasn't sure how each victim played into all this, but she would find out. She was determined to, because there was a rhyme and a reason to this case. Charli was more sure of that than ever before.

"Matt, could you pull up those photos of Haley Reed's sign-in sheets? I want to take a look at them."

Matthew dug in his pocket and produced his phone. "Here you go."

"Thanks." Charli took her time studying each picture, zooming in and swiping to the left until she got to the last photo. She handed it back. "Mind printing them off?"

He gave her a little salute. "Yes, ma'am."

While she waited, she logged into Haley's case to see if any photos or evidence had been uploaded yet. She was in luck. Twenty-six images were included in the file. Many more would be uploaded as the case progressed, but this was a start.

Taking deep breaths, Charli clicked through each one. She was about to click out of the final picture when something caught her eye. From the angle the crime tech captured the shot, light glinted from a small object that was located about six inches from the victim's face.

Clicking back to a close-up image, Charli was able to understand what it was.

A penny.

Something niggled in her brain. What was it? And did it matter? After all, loose change present at a crime scene wasn't an evidentiary burning bush.

Backing out of Haley's file, Charli located Pastor Layne's case. Clicking it open, she went straight to the crime scene photos...and there it was.

Another penny. This one was also just a few inches from the dead man's head. Granted, she also spotted a dime and what looked like a tarnished nickel in a wider shot, but still...

Sitting up straighter, she opened Gretta Franklin's file. This time, a copper sphere was near her right shoulder.

"This could mean nothing," she told herself as an image of Roger Stanton appeared on her screen.

And there it was. As shiny as all the others.

Did it mean anything?

The door opened and Matthew came into the office, a small stack of paper in his hand. "They just called a briefing. We need to get to the conference room now."

She looked up at him, her mouth hanging open a bit. "Matt..."

He frowned at her. "What?"

Dazed, Charli glanced back at the screen. "I'm not sure, but I might have found a connection between the victims."

26

Charli's full attention was trained on Special Agent Jay Brady as he stood at the front of the conference room, a smartboard glowing behind him. He'd been running through different slides containing relevant information about the case, including rundowns of all the victims.

They were just finishing up with Haley Reed's slide, which was a little bare due to her lack of familial connections. As it turned out, she didn't have much of a social media presence either. She had a Facebook page, but that was seldom used, as well as a LinkedIn profile.

Charli was itching to tell the team about her theory regarding the pennies, but she hesitated. She needed to think the discovery through a little bit more.

Joining Charli and Matthew around the conference table were Ruth, several other detectives, and numerous FBI and GBI agents. Much to Charli's chagrin, Janice Piper was seated across from Matthew, smiling at him like a hyena ready to jump its prey. Thankfully, in a room this crowded, it was easy to ignore the way the detective salivated over Charli's partner.

"Right before this meeting, I heard from ballistics, and they've concluded the bullet that killed Haley Reed is from a Glock 19, the same as our other three victims. They're in the process of comparing striations to see if there is a match between the three drive-by shootings and the shooting of Haley Reed."

It was going to be a match, Charli knew it.

Brady flipped to a new slide. "I've had a team combing security camera footage, and no Honda Accord was located so far."

Charli wasn't really that surprised. "He could have dumped the vehicle due to the increased scrutiny on that make and model."

Brady nodded. "Or he knows the area so well that he was able to avoid being caught on camera. The unsub has been doing a decent job at throwing us off."

Or he could have walked.

Or rode the damn bus.

Or tunneled in like Bugs Bunny from back in the days.

Charli pressed her lips together so that she wouldn't make any of those suggestions out loud.

"What about tonight?" Preston Powell flipped a page in a thick folder in front of him. "Were we able to find any footage around the school?"

"We have, but we haven't been able to identify an unknown subject at this time. Again, he could know the area well enough to avoid detection." Keeping his attention on Preston, Brady asked, "Have we secured Haley Reed's prior sign-in sheets yet?" Brady slid his hands behind his back and clasped them together, his posture still rigid. *I'd be willing to bet a hundred bucks this guy was in the military.*

"We have people searching at her apartment, and I'm waiting to hear from the state to determine if she provides those types of records to them. I've also requested the contact information of all support group leaders within the city." He glanced at his watch. "I'm guessing we won't hear back until the morning."

Janice lifted a hand. "I think we should provide officers at other support groups. I just think that—"

Brady held up a hand, apparently not needing to hear more. "Do you also think we should provide security at every mini-mart, radiation department, and church?"

If looks could kill, Janice could set the whole room ablaze. Her normally pale complexion took on a ruddy tone. Charli almost felt sorry for the detective. *Almost.*

Preston, sensing the growing tension, leaned forward. "I understand your line of thinking, Detective Piper. I appreciate that you want to protect as many people as possible, but we need to focus on the city at large."

Brady broke in. "We still have no idea if we're all going to wake up tomorrow to another drive-by shooting of a random citizen, so I want our forces out on the street. People are fearful that they're going to be the next randomized target. It's our job to make them feel like we're doing everything we can to make sure that doesn't happen."

Charli couldn't hold on to her theory any longer.

"I think the victims are connected." She cleared her throat as all eyes turned her way. "Detective Church and I examined the crime scene photos before this briefing, and I think we've found something of interest." She pulled out a stack of photos from a folder on the table and spread them out. "At each crime scene, there's a penny near the victim's head or upper torso. That could be enough to connect—"

A bark of laughter cut her off. It came from an agent from Brady's team, a stout fellow with jet-black hair. "Sounds like one of the plots from my wife's cozy mystery novels." He drew out every syllable in an exaggerated Southern accent. "She likes to read those corny books before we go to sleep. It bugs the ever-loving crap out of me."

Beside her, Matthew growled low in his throat while Charli balled up her fists under the table.

Whatever you say, Agent Deliverance.

"Since I only read true crimes about serial killers, I'm not getting the cozy mystery analogy." Charli took a deep breath and forced her hands to relax. "If you'll open your mind a little, you'll see what I'm talking about. In the three initial murders, it makes sense that loose change could be scattered on the pavement where the victims fell." She lifted the picture of Haley up. "But in a gymnasium? What are the odds?" Charli returned her focus on Jay Brady. "I want to see if those pennies were collected into evidence. And if they were, I suggest we first dust them for prints before we look at them more closely."

Agent Deliverance leaned forward, his hands on his knees, and let out a loud guffaw. "Darlin', you're grasping at straws."

Grasping at straws? Un-freaking-believable.

Charli glanced over at Matthew and winced as steam practically billowed out of his ears. *Uh-oh.* The last thing they needed right now was a blowup. Even if this guy was being a total jackass, Charli was already running through ways to diffuse the situation in her head.

Before Charli had to play referee to a room full of men with egos the size of Texas, Preston Powell held up his phone. "I've got some…interesting news."

Brady rolled his wrist in a "come on" sign. "And?"

If Preston sensed any tension in the room, he didn't show it. The man was a rock, and Charli realized just how well the agent could perform under pressure.

A grin spread across Preston's face, making the corners of

his eyes crinkle. "Apparently, one of the locations for grief counseling groups is at Cornerstone Presbyterian."

Janice Piper's hand flew to her mouth, covering her bright red lipstick. "The same church the minister worked?"

Though the question hadn't been necessary, the room stirred with interest.

Brady walked over to a thick folder on the edge of the conference table. "We have a contact at the church, correct? It's..."

"Jeremy Abbott." Charli pulled out her phone. "We can call him right now. It's late, and he may not answer, but..."

Brady gave a curt nod. "Doesn't matter. Call him. At the rate this unsub is going, we could have another death before the sun rises. The city isn't sleeping, and neither is this killer. And while you're at it, go ahead and see if those pennies were bagged as evidence, and if so, run them for prints." He turned his dark eyes on Agent Deliverance. "Excellent observation, Detective Cross."

Agent Deliverance sank back into his seat. Charli was glad she wasn't on the receiving end of Brady's pointed stare.

Once Matthew and Charli exited the conference room, Preston slipped out right behind them and handed Charli his phone. "You need to see this. I was emailed a list of the locations with their flyers. They all advertise different types of grief counseling. And the one at Cornerstone Presbyterian is specifically religious."

Charli held it up between her and Matthew. The flyer listed the day and time of the group as Saturday at five p.m., advertising the meeting as *a spiritual approach to dealing with grief*. Listed activities were group prayer, guidance from a licensed counselor, open sharing, and prayer cards.

Matthew zoomed in on the flyer. "What the hell is a prayer card?"

"I don't know." Preston rubbed his chin as he read over Charli's shoulder. "I'm not a religious man myself."

Charli handed Preston back his phone before dialing Jeremy Abbott on her own. She wouldn't consider herself all that religious either, but she found herself saying a silent prayer in her head that he'd answer.

"Hello, Detective Cross?" The hoarseness in Jeremy's voice confirmed that he'd been sleeping.

Thank you. Thank you. Thank you.

"Hi, Jeremy. I'm sorry to wake you, but I have an urgent question regarding our case."

There was a yawn at the other end of the line. "You never have to apologize for calling, Detective. I've been following the case on the news. I can see how dire the situation is getting, and I want to do everything I can to help."

Charli tapped the speakerphone button so Matthew and Preston could both hear. "Thank you, I appreciate that. Do you know anything about the grief counseling sessions that occur at the church? There are several other locations for the sessions, including a local high school gym."

"Well, I don't run them, and I typically don't attend them, but I have been at the church when they occur."

Where did Charli even begin with these questions? So many were running through her head. "Do you know who runs them?"

"A group called Reclaim Recovery sends out their counselors, I believe. It's in coordination with the city. They often send out different people, so I don't have a name for you. If you'd like, I can reach out to the group or give you their contact information."

Charli didn't hesitate. "Let's do both. Give me their information but try to get in touch with them as well." Sometimes, it was easier for someone who was already connected with an organization to get answers.

"Will do. Not sure if they have anyone manning the phone this late, but I'll leave a message and then follow up first thing."

It was probably the best she could ask for at this point. "Thank you. Much appreciated. Can you text their information to me?"

Her phone buzzed in her hand. "Already sent."

Charli appreciated promptness. "Got it. Do you know what these groups are about specifically?"

"Hmm…I'm pretty sure they are open to anyone who is grieving for any reason. They could be grieving the loss of a loved one or even grieving their own terminal illness. Sometimes, when a loved one is in the process of dying, family members attend the sessions for additional support. The group is very open to anyone who wants to join."

Charli closed her eyes as she took in everything Jeremy was saying. "Can you run me through what happens in an average meeting?"

A muffled yawn came through the phone, and Charli stifled one of her own. "Sure. It opens up with a group prayer. The administrator will speak a bit about a theme of that week. It could be anything from letting God guide you through grief to acceptance of death. Sometimes, the topics are religious, and sometimes they're more general to the experience of grief. After that, the attendees are free to talk about whatever is on their minds."

Charli pulled up the flyer on her phone as Jeremy was speaking. She fixated on two words. "And what about prayer cards? What exactly are those used for?"

"Oh, they're something we try to do here at Cornerstone Presbyterian. Because people don't always feel free to share their prayer requests in a public setting, we have prayer cards located in every pew. People are free to write down their prayers and leave them in our box, with the promise that the minister would be reading them."

"Do people sign their names to these cards?" This could be a long shot, but it couldn't hurt to ask.

"Many are anonymous, but yes…sometimes. Why?"

Well, sometimes was better than nothing. "I know this may be intrusive, but it would be supremely helpful if we could look at those prayer cards. Do you guys keep them?"

"Of course. I can run down to the church right now if you think they're relevant to the case."

Charli needed every available tool in her arsenal. "That would be great. Thank you so much."

A muffled shuffling sound came through the other end of the line. "I'm getting dressed as we speak. Let me just get off the phone, and I'll—"

"Wait. I have one more question for you. Is the name Haley Reed familiar?"

Jeremy made a humming noise. "No, I don't believe I know anyone by that name. Why do you ask?"

"I'm not at liberty to say, and I'd appreciate if you could keep that name between us for the time being."

"Of course, Detective. I'll let you know when I get a hold of those prayer cards."

Even if the prayer cards didn't lead them to their killer, Charli couldn't help but believe they were at least taking a step in the right direction.

"Thank you for your help. I really appreciate it." Charli disconnected the call and massaged her temples before glancing between Preston and Matthew. "Well, it may not be the strongest link, but with Cornerstone Presbyterian popping up again, maybe it'll be something else to tie our victims together."

Matthew flashed her a cheeky grin. "I don't know, Charli.

Using prayer cards to solve a homicide? Sounds a little bit like a cozy murder mystery to me."

Preston threw back his head and laughed. "Good one."

Charli watched the two men relax together for the first time. Maybe the two could end up being friends.

She gave herself a mental shake. Why exactly did she care if these two became buddies?

I don't.

With that mental affirmation, she refocused on the case. "So, Haley Reed may not ring a bell for Jeremy, but that doesn't mean she didn't have a connection with the church or the minister himself. We need to ask someone closer to the minister if they know of Ms. Reed."

Matthew glanced at his watch. "It's the wee hours of the morning. I know that Brady says we need to be working around the clock, but I'm not about to wake a sleeping widow. That woman was barely holding herself together in the daytime."

Charli couldn't agree more. Even if they could get in touch with Mrs. Layne, they needed her functional to ask her questions.

"First thing in the morning." She yawned. "Well, later this morning, we'll get in contact with her. For now, let's see if those pennies were bagged and tagged."

27

Charli rubbed the muscles in her aching neck. She'd developed a crick from where she'd fallen asleep at her desk.

Disgusted at her body for needing a few hours rest, she scowled at her computer screen. No new messages. At least no message she'd been hoping for.

No compilation of Haley Reed's sign-in sheets.

No Honda Accord on the traffic camera footage.

No pennies collected as evidence. Well, to be fair, they were still logging each piece of evidence, so they just might not be in the system yet.

On the bright side, there also hadn't been another murder.

Charli stretched out her arms and let out a loud yawn, causing Matthew's head to jolt upward, a piece of paper stuck to his cheek.

He rubbed his still closed eyes. "I'm up, I'm up!"

"You and that paper both, apparently." Charli yawned a second time. "I'm going to go grab a coffee. You want anything?"

Matthew swiped at the paper. "Sure, I'll take the strongest you can find with extra cream and sugar please."

Charli was in the process of groaning her way to her feet when her phone rang. "Detective Cross speaking." Plopping back down into her chair, she leaned her head on her palm.

"Detective, I think I've found something you might want to see."

At the sound of Jeremy Abbott's voice, Charli's head jerked up. "What's that?"

"Could you and your partner meet me at the church?"

She was already on her feet, with no groaning this time. "Absolutely. We'll be right over." Charli hung up and turned to Matthew. "Put on your game face because there's no time for coffee."

Matthew groaned, but Charli didn't need caffeine anymore. A potential break in the case got her adrenaline going. It was enough to wake her up, but Matthew trudged his way toward the parking lot.

There were still a few news vans parked out front, but not nearly as many reporters as the day before, and Charli and Matthew were able to exit through the back entrance and get into her car without interruption.

The ride over was silent, but that was just fine with Charli since a million gears were turning in her head. What could Jeremy have found for her? Did he find something related to Haley Reed? Or could it really be that the prayer cards held some information?

Charli half-jogged into the church after she exited the car, Matthew following close behind. They found Jeremy in the front pew with his head down, staring at something in his hand.

"Everything all right?" Charli stood while Matthew took a seat in the pew next to him.

"No...I'm sorry, but I'm not sure if it is." He raised his

hand, displaying some white index cards. "I've spent the last few hours since you called reading through prayer cards. As I said, most were anonymous. And most that do have a name attached were very benign. But I noticed repeated prayers from one individual that got increasingly...concerning."

"Concerning how?" Charli pulled on a pair of gloves before reaching for the cards, not that it would do much good. But procedure was procedure.

Jeremy handed them over. "They're in chronological order. We keep the prayer cards in boxes based on the month they were handed in. These are from a person called..." he squinted at the scrawled signature, "Mark? Mary maybe?"

Charli shook her head. "If I had to put money on it, the writing is male. Jackson is definitely the last name and M is the first initial." She willed the scribble to make sense. It didn't. "I just can't tell."

Matthew stood up to read over Charli's shoulder. "Lucky for us, he printed the message before signing the card."

The first two messages didn't seem too out of the ordinary.

Need prayer for better health.

I pray for the strength to deal with what is ahead of me.

The third wasn't too odd either.

Please, Lord, give me a good diagnosis. I don't want to leave my wife alone.

But the more they read, the more erratic the prayers became.

Prayer is a waste of breath. Why haven't any of mine been answered?

There is no God. There are no answered prayers.

Want a penny for my thoughts? Here you go...you peddle lies. Is all this talk of miracles a bunch of shit?

Want a prayer? I pray that I can listen to the man who's been inside me all along.

Charli focused on the second to last message. *Penny for my thoughts?* Was there a connection?

"Well, this guy seems like he's losing it." Matthew put on his own gloves before taking the cards.

Charli turned to Jeremy as Matthew read through them once more. "Do you know anyone who might fit the M Jackson name?"

"No, I don't, and there is no way to know when exactly he dropped off these prayer cards. As I said, they're organized by month." Jeremy tapped a folder labeled "September."

Charli nodded at the stack of other folders beside the current one. "Did you check all the months?"

Jeremy nodded. "Sure did. Nothing that looked like these, though."

Matthew bagged the cards. "So, this M Jackson fellow could have visited the church on Sunday, or he could have attended the grief group?"

Jeremy pursed his lips. "Exactly. And I must say, I know all our regular members fairly well. But it could be that this person was using a fake name. Or perhaps they were a relative of one of our churchgoers. People do bring in friends and family."

These cards could be important. *Penny for my thoughts?*

"Have you heard back from the Reclaim Recovery group?"

Jeremy shook his head at Charli's question, his shoulders sinking. "I'm still waiting to hear back from them."

Charli snapped the gloves off. "We can stop by Mrs. Layne's home on our way back to the precinct to see if she has any knowledge about Haley Reed or this M Jackson person."

"Wait, you don't have to go by the minister's house." Jeremy pointed toward a door. "Mrs. Layne is in her husband's office."

"Right now?" The dark bags under Matthew's eyes seemed to have lightened at the news.

"Yes. She's been spending a lot of time in there since Pastor Layne's...death." Jeremy sighed as he rubbed an eye with his fist. "I leave her alone when she's in that room. I think it's her time to connect with Victor, and I don't want to bother her."

Unfortunately, Charli and Matthew didn't have the luxury of time. Plus, if she was awake and at the church, perhaps she'd be functional enough to question.

Jeremy directed them to the minister's office door, which was closed. Matthew knocked three times, and a hoarse voice came from inside. "Come in."

Mrs. Layne was curled up on an emerald velvet loveseat in the corner of the room. She had a white blanket wrapped around her, pulled up to her neck.

"Hello, Mrs. Layne. I'm Detective Cross with my partner, Detective Church. We spoke at your home before."

The veins in the widow's eyes were a bright crimson red. As tired and grief-stricken as she appeared, she seemed to be more aware of their presence this time.

"Hello, Detectives. I apologize, but I don't remember much of our encounter." She forced herself to sit up, and her elbow trembled as she used one arm to propel her forward.

"We completely understand." Matthew let the door shut behind them and sat in one of the armchairs in front of the minister's desk. "And we're sorry to bother you again while you're grieving, but we have a couple important questions to ask you."

She tucked her unruly hair behind her ears. "Okay."

Charli perched on one of the chairs between the desk and Mrs. Layne. "Are you familiar with a woman named Haley Reed?"

Mrs. Layne furrowed her brow and opened her mouth, pausing before she spoke. "What does Haley Reed have to do with this?"

Charli and Matthew exchanged glances.

Matthew rested his elbows on his knees. "Are you saying you do know Ms. Reed?"

Mrs. Layne's fingers fidgeted with the edge of the blanket. "Yes. She's been working with the grief group we hold at the church for a month. Why?"

Charli gripped the edge of her seat. *Please be the connection we need.* "And what group is this?"

"I forget the exact name. I know it has the word 'recovery' in it, though." Mrs. Layne tucked her blanket onto her lap, smoothing out the wrinkles. "I just don't understand. Why are you so concerned with the grief group? What does that have to do with Victor's death? The news has made it seem that he died in a random shooting."

Charli wanted to kick a couple reporters in the ass. "The media isn't always the most informed on the latest developments of the case, and it's too early to say that your husband's death was random at all. These questions will help us determine that."

As if this information breathed life into the widow, Mrs. Layne's pale cheeks warmed to a rosy pink. "I remember the name of the group. It's Reclaim Recovery. We were having some issues with the program and the fact that they were constantly sending out new therapists. Victor attended the meetings and didn't think the attendees benefited as much when they were always speaking to a different individual, so he contacted the city to see if they could provide someone who would be consistent. They sent Haley Reed."

Hope soared in Charli's chest. They were finally making a few connections.

First the pennies and now this.

Even if it didn't lead them directly to the shooter, just the information that these killings weren't random was invaluable. That knowledge would go a long way to putting the public's mind at ease while giving them more investigative threads to pull.

"Did you meet Haley Reed?" Charli sat up straight in her chair, her legs trembling with anticipation. All the exhaustion she'd experienced this morning had fled.

Mrs. Layne brushed a few strands of hair off her cheek. "No, but Victor said she seemed to be a competent counselor."

Even Matthew seemed wide awake now. "What can you tell us about Haley Reed and your husband's relationship?"

Mrs. Layne's mouth dropped open. "Relationship? Victor only spoke of her once or twice, so I wouldn't call it a relationship. I remember Victor telling me that Ms. Reed was a compassionate soul."

Charli's pen flew across the page. No doubt, Agent Brady was going to want every detail of this conversation. "Do you know of a man with the first initial of M and the last name of Jackson?"

Mrs. Layne's brow furrowed in concentration. She paused for a moment before shaking her head. "I'm sorry, that name doesn't ring a bell. Is that another counselor?"

"No, it isn't." Charli wasn't going to explain where they got the name. They didn't even know who this Jackson person was yet, let alone if he had any involvement in the case. Charli would never reveal the name of a person of interest to the loved one of a victim unless she was positive they were on the right track.

If she did, that might cause that loved one to take justice into their own hands. Not that Mrs. Layne seemed to be the vigilante type, but she was certainly distressed about the death of her husband. It was impossible to know what someone might do under that kind of pressure.

And for all Charli knew, this M Jackson was just an innocent citizen. Sure, the prayer cards seemed unhinged, but most people struggling with their mental health weren't murderers. And the worst thing this man seemed to have done thus far was claim the church was dishonest. Plenty of people reached that conclusion about religious institutions every day. They weren't all ravenous with rage, though.

Although Charli had already given Mrs. Layne her business card, she handed her another one. In the state she'd been in, who knew if she even remembered where that small slip of paper was.

"If you remember anything else about Haley Reed or think of anything else that you'd like us to know, would you give us a call?"

Mrs. Layne rubbed her hand across her face. "But I still don't know what she has to do with this. You think she killed my Victor?"

Haley's name had not yet been disclosed to the public, so Charli certainly couldn't announce her death. "No, we don't believe she harmed Victor in any way, but we aren't at liberty to disclose more information at this point."

Mrs. Layne dropped her head into her hands, her hair a stringy mess. Had she even brushed it in the last few days? But Charli couldn't blame her. After Madeline died, simple tasks like taking a shower had been an effort.

"I just feel like I'm getting no information. My husband is dead, and nobody but me seems to care! When is someone going to tell me something?" With her head still in her hands, Mrs. Layne's voice was muffled, but her angry tone was clear.

Charli didn't mind this frustration one bit. If anything, she was happy Mrs. Layne could feel anger at the moment.

To move from sadness to anger was all a part of the healing process, and Charli and Matthew could certainly handle any rage she wanted to toss at them. That was just part of the job.

"I promise that we care deeply about this. We've got the FBI on this case, Mrs. Layne. We're using all our resources."

Mrs. Layne raised her head, the corners of her lips turned down. "Really?"

"Absolutely. My partner and I slept at the office last night. We're working nonstop to find who is responsible for your husband's death. If you don't feel you're getting a lot of communication from us, just know that it's because we're focused on finding your husband's murderer."

After leaving Mrs. Layne to continue to grieve alone, they said goodbye to Jeremy on their way out to the car.

Charli didn't even wait until she reached the vehicle before she called into the precinct. She wanted a list of every male Jackson with the first name beginning with M as soon as possible. They also needed a handwriting expert who might be able to decipher that first name. She shot a text to Preston Powell, asking if he'd gotten Haley Reed's sign-in sheets yet.

I haven't. I'll give them a call again to try to push this through.

Thank you. Headed to the precinct. Be there soon.

Matthew still had the cards in his hand when he got into the car, and Charli nodded toward the glove box as she flashed him a cheeky grin. "Put those babies in a safe place."

"I'll guard them with my life." Matthew held the cards to his heart for a moment before putting them in the glove box. "You really think this could be our guy?"

"I don't know." Charli really had no idea. "There's one thing I'm certain of, though. This is not a set of random murders. There is a clear connection between Haley Reed and Victor Layne. That cannot possibly just be a coincidence."

Even if M Jackson had nothing to do with the case, this break was huge. Ruth was going to be awash with relief when she learned this newest development.

But the reality was, the killer was still out there, and they had no idea who his next victim would be.

28

Charli hung over Matthew's shoulder. "Well?"

"I've gone through every Jackson in Savannah with M as a first initial and haven't yet found one listed as an owner of a Honda or a Glock 19." Matthew put his head in his hands as he hunched over his computer.

Charli's heart sank in her chest.

Crap.

She'd been hoping Jackson would be the proud owner of both a Honda and a Glock, giving them compelling evidence for a warrant. But since he—on paper at least—owned neither, she was back to square one.

It wasn't impossible, though. Charli's gaze flitted to the doorway. She had texted Preston to meet her in her office immediately. Surely by now he had a list of Haley Reed's groups and those who attended them. Charli was beyond ready to get her hands on that list.

Clunky footsteps reverberated off the hallway walls and into their office, and Charli turned toward the door.

Preston waltzed in with three coffees in hand. "I'm assuming you two are as tired as I am. I only slept like—"

Charli jumped up from her chair. "Did you hear back about the lists yet?"

She didn't need coffee. She needed answers. This new break in the case had given her more of a boost than caffeine ever could.

Preston's eyes widened a bit. "Well, good morning to you too, Charli. Coffee?"

Charli flashed him an impatient smile and nodded. "Good morning. Sorry, I just need to know if we have that list. Thanks for the caffeine."

Charli glanced over at Matthew, who was staring at Preston just as intently. With their gazes burning a hole in the back of his head, Preston set the cardboard tray on his temporary desk.

Preston glanced from Charli to Matthew as he picked up his coffee. "Okay, what am I missing here?"

Matthew rolled his chair to Preston's makeshift desk and grabbed one of the drinks. "Have you not spoken to Brady yet?"

"No. I just got in. You two are the first people I'm seeing. What's going on?"

A burst of excitement shot through Charli. "We've got a name." She scratched her nose. "Well...sort of."

Preston's entire countenance shifted from casual to interested in an instant. "Tell me everything."

Charli pulled up a photo of the prayer cards on her phone and flashed it to the agent. "Both the Cornerstone church and the grief support groups that meet there collect these prayer cards, and Jeremy Abbott files them away by month. We've got increasingly disturbing messages from a person we believe might be a man called M Jackson. The first name is a scrawl that we're hoping a handwriting expert can decipher. I'm also hoping the expert can confirm it's a man's handwriting. Oh...and guess who was hosting those support groups?"

Preston glanced up from where he was reading and shot her a small grin. "Haley Reed."

Give that GBI agent a prize. "Exactly. Haley Reed."

Preston handed Charli back her phone. "Run me through your thought process."

Charli tapped her screen. "I'm thinking that we have someone who is very sick connected to Cornerstone. This person digressed from feeling positive to seemingly blaming someone or multiple someones for 'peddling lies' about there being a god who might save him."

Preston stared at the wall past her shoulder, and Charli could practically see his mind working to connect the dots. "Keep going."

Heartened that he wasn't shooting her theory down, Charli walked to the murder board and made a note. "Haley was clearly targeted. Is that because she's one of the people 'peddling lies'? Was the pastor also 'peddling lies'? Was Gretta doing so as a hospital employee?"

Preston held out both hands in a *slow-down* motion. "Playing devil's advocate...our note writer could just be another churchgoer. He sounds unhinged, sure. Plenty of people are, though. Does a M Jackson in the Savannah area own a Glock 19 or a Honda? Is he on Gretta's patient list?"

"We don't know. The radiology list hasn't been uploaded in the files yet so we're sitting on our thumbs waiting for a copy." Matthew popped the lid of his coffee cup off, so he could drink from the cup instead of the little hole in the top of the lid. "We have established that there is no M Jackson registered to a Glock 19 or Honda, though."

Charli lifted a hand. If Preston could play devil's advocate, so could she. "Which doesn't mean squat for a lot of people. Car and gun could be stolen or registered to a spouse or friend."

Preston nodded. "He's absolutely someone to look into. I just don't want to get ahead of ourselves. I know this case is driving everyone wild. We're on the edge of our seats waiting to see if our shooter will strike again, but we still have a lot of digging to do." He gazed directly into Charli's eyes. "What's your plan?"

Charli let go of the breath it felt like she'd been holding since the first day of this case.

He believed her. Trusted her. But he was also right. They couldn't get ahead of themselves.

But deep in her gut, she knew she was onto something. Not that she'd ever confess to Matthew that she'd let her instincts rule her decisions.

Charli whipped out her notepad to jot down her list. "We need to talk to every M Jackson in Savannah and the surrounding counties. I'll go through a preliminary list and dole out assignments for which of our officers will visit whom."

Preston started typing on his phone. "I'll have that list to you in five minutes or less."

Enjoying having a GBI agent as her secretary, even for a moment, Charli processed through everything else she could get his team to do. "Do you have a handwriting expert we can send images of the notes to?"

"Yes. Forward them to me and I'll get it done."

A few taps on her phone later and she checked that task off her list. There were plenty more. "We need Gretta Franklin's patient records uploaded pronto, and we need someone to interview as many members of the grief support group as possible. Maybe one of them remembers an M Jackson. We need to go through Haley Reed's files and see if she has any addresses or phone numbers."

Preston nodded along as he continued to type. "What time do you want to set up a team briefing?"

He was asking her? Pleased, Charli glanced at the clock. "Eight a.m. sharp. The second we locate our M Jackson, we'll need SWAT." She glanced at Matthew. "Can you put them on standby?"

Matthew shot her a little salute. "Yes, ma'am."

Charli grinned, but only for a second. They were going to catch the bastard terrorizing the people of her city.

Today.

29

Listening to my police scanner, I dropped my head into my hands. The cops weren't exactly saying they knew the identity of the Savannah Sniper, which was what the media was calling me, but there was a new excitement in the way they were chatting with each other.

They were getting closer. I could feel it.

When one of the officers confirmed that he'd arrived at 456 Ash Street, and the dispatcher advised him to "use caution," a quick google search of that address showed that the home belonged to a Mark Jackson.

A few minutes later, another officer radioed in that he had arrived at 916 Reynolds Lane. I googled the address and nearly gasped out loud. Martin Jackson.

They knew my name. How?

"Because you fucked something up."

Not interested in Damian's narration right then, I ignored his commentary about as successfully as I ignored the pain he created in my abdomen. How many Martin Jacksons were in Savannah? How much longer did I have?

Damian was right, though. The past few days had become

foggy, and I was living in a blur. I must have done something to tip them off.

With a groan, I willed my aching body to get up and peek through the small garage window. When I didn't spot any police cars from that vantage point, I headed inside the house. In the living room, I gingerly lifted up the curtain.

At least the cops weren't staking out my house. Yet.

"You're running out of time."

Pressing a fist into my stomach like that would shut Damian up, I paced the room. "Don't you think I know that?"

"How are you going to pull this off?"

I had no idea. "I'll make it happen."

"But what if—"

Slamming my fist through the living room wall, I screamed, rejoicing in a different kind of pain. A pain not connected with my cancer. "Just shut the hell up!"

I was sick of Damian controlling my life and telling me what to do. Wasn't it bad enough that he was killing me? I cursed that damn counselor Haley for suggesting I name my cancer.

"Talk to it," she'd said. "Make it a person instead of a monster."

Her suggestion had done the exact opposite.

Heavy footsteps padded down the hallway. "Honey, are you okay?"

I whipped around to face my wife, my bruised knuckles seeking another source to punch. *Not yet.*

"I'm fine."

With trembling fingers, she tucked a loose strand of stringy hair behind her ear. "I heard yelling. Are you sure nothing's wrong?"

In a few quick strides, I closed the gap between us, not stopping until my face was only a few inches from hers. Couldn't she see how sick I was? Couldn't she tell that the "man she loved" was dying? Couldn't she see the truth of it in my eyes?

"I don't know what you're talking about."

She took two steps back, raising a hand to cover her mouth. Her eyes flicked up and down my body, like they were an x-ray scan she could use to see inside of me.

I pressed a hand to my belly. Do you see this? Do you? *Please. See me.*

If she provided even a little hint that she knew me as well as she always said she did, I might let her live.

She frowned. "W-what happened to your hand? Did you break it? It looks so swollen."

Deflated, I glanced down at my hand, and a wave of dizziness went through me. She was right. My right hand was twice the size of my left. As if that acknowledgement made the injury real, pain began to pulse in my knuckles. With a groan, I flexed my fingers and winced. I could barely move it.

How had that happened?

"Honey?" She rested a hand on my arm, and I yanked away from her touch.

"I don't know." It was the truth.

The shiver of fear that ran down my spine wasn't from the idea of getting arrested. That was the least of my concerns now. And it wasn't even from the thought of not being able to finish what I'd started.

I had no idea how I'd broken my hand, and I was terrified. A haze of confusion permeated my mind, and I swayed as the room spun around me.

"Honey," an arm snaked around my shoulder and steadied me, "why don't you sit down? Your breakfast is ready. I'll get some ice for your hand and bring your food to you in here. Just relax." She guided me to the sofa, and I sat there in a haze.

What was happening to me? Why couldn't I think

straight? Pain shot up my arm, and I cradled the swollen mess with my left hand. How the hell was I supposed to carry out my plan if I could barely move my fingers? I couldn't shoot with my left hand if my life depended on it.

"You did it on purpose."

What was Damian suggesting? That I'd purposefully injured myself so I'd be forced to stop the killing?

"That's ridiculous."

Was it, though?

Was I losing my nerve now that I was close to being caught?

"You're going to have to fix that hole in the wall, you know?"

My wife's shrill voice from the kitchen was the exact wake-up call I needed. Wasn't it clear to her that I was going through something terrible? And what does she do? Provide loving support? No, she continued to nag.

Fueled with a new infusion of rage, I pushed myself up from the couch. With my head still spinning, I stumbled to the bathroom to splash cold water on my face. Once there, I stopped in front of the mirror, my reflection startling me.

Who was this gaunt shell of a man with a sickly yellow hue?

Damian's sarcastic laughter vibrated deep inside.

Turning away from the mirror, I rummaged around the medicine cabinet until I found an elastic bandage. Plopping down on the toilet seat, I struggled to wrap my balloon of a hand.

Finally finished, I opened the linen closet and dug around for my stash of painkillers the doctor had prescribed. Nah, taking them would only make me less coherent, and I needed to be on high alert. I was already a mess as it was.

"What are you doing in there?"

If that bitch nagged me one more time...

Gritting my teeth, I squeezed my eyes shut before coming out of the bathroom. With measured steps, I followed my nose to the living room. My blood sugar was dropping, and I needed to eat something soon. "Coming."

To give her credit, my wife had gone through some effort with breakfast, and the food looked delicious on the tray she'd centered on the coffee table. I felt a moment of gratitude. I had loved her once, after all. "Thank you."

She set the tray in my lap. "Penny for your thoughts?"

The two coins left in my pocket grew heavier. I hated that expression. "Trust me, you don't want to know what I'm thinking right now."

She sighed, loud and long. "After you eat, I'm taking you to the emergency room. You need to get that—"

"No!" I slammed my left hand down on the tray, and the bowl of grits went flying, splattering the sloppy mixture all over the couch and floor. I drew in a deep breath, forcing myself to remain calm.

"Martin! What the hell is wrong with you?"

I shoved a piece of toast in my mouth, biting off half of the slice and chewing like I hadn't eaten in years. "I wrapped it up. It's just swollen, but it's fine. I'll be fine." I glanced at the clock. "Don't you need to be at work?" A forkful of eggs wasn't quite as easy to manage, and most of them dropped back onto the plate as my left hand attempted to get them to my mouth.

Damn. What I wouldn't give to be ambidextrous right now.

"I took the day off." She licked her thin lips. "I thought we could talk."

My pulse spiked. Talk?

Jesus no.

I should just kill her now and get it over with. Just because she was the last on my list didn't mean I had to follow that exact order. But how? I couldn't risk the neighbors hearing a gunshot, and with my messed up hand, strangulation wasn't an option.

Damian laughed. *"You fucked up again."*

Hot rage boiled through my veins at the accuracy of his statement. I had fucked up. Even in the face of my death, I still couldn't manage to do things right.

"Except to kill. You're very good at that. Go take care of that heifer now. Get your confidence back."

Yes. Damian was right. I'd feel so much better with her gone. Plus, I might not get another chance because once I left this house, I doubted I'd ever be back.

I could use a knife, watch her blood spill from her throat. Maybe cut out her tongue.

I didn't even realize that she'd left the room until her voice rang from down the hall. "I'm going to run to the store. I'll clean your mess up when I get back."

A few moments later, the front door clicked. She was gone. At least for a little while.

"You missed your chance."

Think. Think. Think.

Giving up on the fork, I shoveled more food into my mouth with my fingers. I wasn't hungry but I needed the nourishment the breakfast provided. I had a big day ahead of me, I knew.

Should I wait until she returned? Surprise her with the knife while she unpacked the groceries?

"You don't have time to wait."

Damian was right. The police could be at my doorstep at any time. How many Martin Jacksons lived in Savannah, after all?

Fueled with food and caffeine, I peeked out of the front window again. Still no cops. At least none that I could see. I lurched to the back door and inched up the shade. No cops in sight there either.

What if they were hiding somewhere?

"You need to leave."

But how?

I'd hidden the Accord, and even if I hadn't, I didn't dare drive it in public. The wife had just taken the CRV because she thought the Accord was in the shop.

"Go out the back. Scale the fence. Get away."

Damian was right, and I felt the urgency in his suggestion to my marrow.

Gathering my gun and extra ammo, I tossed it in the briefcase I used to carry for work. Keeping my head on a swivel, I went through the back door and hopped—well, struggled—over my neighbor's fence to get onto the next street. With my weakened body and useless right hand, it was an act of Congress to make it over, but somehow, I managed. From there, I ordered an Uber.

It would be trackable later. I knew that. When the police were looking for evidence of why I'd done this, the Uber would make it obvious.

I didn't give a rat's ass.

What could they do to a dying man? Give me the death sentence? I snickered at the thought. I was going to be dead before the court trial finished. My only reason to hide before was so that I'd have enough time to pick off everyone on my list. Now that I was pretty sure I was already being followed, there was no reason to hide.

In an interesting twist of fate, the car that pulled up to get me was a silver Honda.

Great.

For a moment, I could only stare at it. It wasn't as old as my car, but it wasn't one of the newer models. If I was the kind of guy who went looking for signs, perhaps I'd find one here.

The driver's side window rolled down. "Man, not this again! I already had two riders turn me down. Look, I swear I'm not the shooter, okay! Just a guy trying to make a buck." His words came out in a hoarse Italian accent. Paired with his gelled black hair and gesticulating hands, the middle-aged man was a walking stereotype.

I grinned at him. "I don't think you're the killer, man. And I'm not canceling the ride."

The driver mimed a dramatic wipe of his forehead. "Phew, you don't know how I need the money."

Poor schmuck. That was me before I completely ghosted my job. Constantly worrying about money, obsessing over my salary and whether it was going to pay the bills. The process was completely emasculating. At least I'd be out of that rat race soon.

When I shut the car door behind me, he started to pull out into the street.

"So, to the hospital, huh? Are you visiting family?"

"No, actually, I'm getting treated there." I didn't bother pulling my seat belt on. What the hell was I trying to protect myself from, anyway?

"Treated? Hey, you ain't gonna get me sick, are ya?" The smile reflected in the rearview mirror was teasing.

"As far as I know, cancer isn't contagious." I tossed my head back, folding my arms in my lap.

The car went dead silent for a moment. It was a shocking thing to say. And early in my illness, I probably would've thought twice before being so blunt with a stranger. Back then, I worked hard to make the people around me more comfortable.

Not anymore, though. There was no reason for pleasantries. I didn't know this guy, and I didn't owe him a thing.

He sucked in a long breath of air. "Sorry, man, I was just teasing. I had no idea. I need to learn to keep my big mouth shut. I hope your treatment goes well."

"It isn't going well, actually. It's terminal."

Strange how smoothly the words fell out of my mouth now. They were once a brick wall in front of me, blocking my path to greatness. Little did I know, they'd become the gateway to what I hadn't realized I'd always wanted to be.

I wouldn't say I welcomed death now. After all, I was still human. If it was possible to get better, I'd take any opportunity to do so. Since I was terminal, though, I had to accept the cards I'd been dealt. My situation was less than ideal, but I was making the most of what time I had left, one lowlife at a time.

Still, I'd never forget the moment I received the news. Before that, I didn't know it was possible for the room to spin without drinking a drop of alcohol. The whole world cratered around me, like an earthquake that occurred only where I stood.

That earthquake hadn't fazed the doctor, who'd been able to tell me my life was ending without a hint of emotion on his face, as though I was just another item on his to-do list to check off and not a person whose life was being ruined.

I'd stumbled out of that room like a drunk man, only to run into the x-ray tech who worked on me. She'd known my diagnosis as soon as my scans came in but hadn't bothered to mention it to me. Apparently, she wasn't allowed.

At first, I thought her nicer than my doctor. She'd pulled me aside to tell me that her cousin had been diagnosed as terminal as well, but after a hefty amount of prayer, she'd gone into remission. I was handed the contact card for Cornerstone Presbyterian and told they could help me there.

Although I was skeptical, my desperation won out. I went. And I thought perhaps there was some validity to the whole

God thing, like maybe if I did what I believed God would want from me, He'd take away my illness. It felt almost good to have a community rallying around me. The grief group I attended at Cornerstone had provided me with a support system, and I'd had high hopes for some good news.

But with every scan I received, things got worse. There was no improvement whatsoever. I was getting weaker and sicker by the day. I'd even gotten into an experimental clinical trial. Looking back on it now, how had I actually believed it to be the gift I had been asking of the Lord?

When that amounted to nothing, I finally saw the church for what it was. Just another form of emasculation, a place that would control me and force me into a well-behaved box with a shiny red bow on top.

All my life, I'd done what I was told, but what was the point? How had I benefited from working my ass off to make other people happy?

Not in a damn way.

This was by far the worst thing that had ever happened to me, though. Not only was I beaten into submission and fed a false sense of hope, but I'd had the last few months of my life stolen from me.

I was glad it had happened, though. It was my awakening, the final straw. With the camel's back broken, I could now explore the man I was always meant to be.

Now, nobody could stop me, and nobody would. I knew my purpose, and it was to destroy anyone who'd ever harmed me, who'd delivered the news of my demise without a care in the world, who'd given me empty platitudes as if that would somehow make me feel better.

It was actually Damian who'd suggested it all.

He'd told me to take back my power and eliminate everyone who'd told me I needed to cope with imminent death. Anyone who'd ever beaten me down into submission.

If there was a god out there, I had to believe that's what he'd want from me.

The rest of the car ride was silent. I'd clearly made my charismatic Italian driver uncomfortable.

Poor bastard.

I didn't mind, though. The quiet provided me with time to think over what I was about to do next.

End the most important person on my list. Then, if I was very lucky, I would be able to head back to my house and finish off the wife.

"She'll pay either way."

Damian was right. I could almost imagine it now. Once the cops learned of what I'd done, they'd question her for hours. Media would scream questions at her from the lawn, demanding how she didn't know she'd been living with a killer. Her friends and family would back away, not wanting her stink to rub off on them.

That was perfect, even better than a quick death.

Part of me considered ending the driver as I left, but what kind of attention would that draw to myself? I hated the way he was looking at me, eyeing me from the rearview mirror with abject pity. He was a glorified cab driver, and he was judging me? Because of my illness? I was more than he'd ever be. I could wipe that look off his face right now.

"Kill him now. No one will ever be the wiser."

My lips set in a thin, hard line. "I've had enough of your ideas, Damian. Shut the hell up."

The driver glanced in the mirror. Was that fear in his eyes? "What was that, sir?"

A shiver of excitement ran through me. I held this man's life in the palm of my hand, and the knowledge of that power was thrilling. "Nothing. Just talking to myself."

Killing him would only jeopardize my next target.

The driver dropped me off in front of the ER, but that

wasn't where I'd go. The emergency room had a metal detector upon entering, but the cancer clinic did not, so I walked around the right side of the building to meet with my doctor.

The receptionist scrunched her eyebrows at me after I waltzed in, my bum hand swollen underneath the bandage.

"I'm so sorry, sir. I didn't realize you had an appointment today."

Click-clack. Clickety-clack. Her long nails pecked at the keyboard as she searched for my time slot.

"I don't have an appointment, actually. I just really need to see the doctor."

"Oh." She pursed her pouty red lips and an image from my fantasy popped into my mind, but I pushed it away. Why would a doctor ever hire a receptionist that looked like she belonged on an episode of *Baywatch*? "Well, unfortunately, the doctor won't be in for another hour. If you want, I can get you penciled in for an appointment tomorrow morn—"

"No!" My tone was harsher than I'd intended, causing her to jolt upright in her seat. I willed myself to speak in a calm voice, belying the rage building inside me. "I'm sorry. It just has to be today. I've got a new symptom, and I really need some kind of relief."

She swallowed hard, and I could tell there was something in her gut screaming that this was wrong, that the situation was off. I knew because I'd experienced a similar gut feeling right before my diagnosis.

Like many women often do, she ignored her instincts. Her drive to be polite outweighed her feeling that this was a dangerous situation. Not that I minded.

Stupid little bitch.

"Well, you're welcome to wait, but I can't promise the doctor will have much time to talk to you." The way her eyes darted from her computer to me, I knew she was hopeful her warning might be enough to deter me, that I'd walk right back out that door.

For the first time today, my lips curled into a half-smile. "That's fine. I promise I won't take up much of his time."

I patted my pants pocket, checking to ensure the coins were still there. Indeed, they were, and I had one with the good doctor's name on it.

30

After the morning briefing, during which Charli handed out assignments to the teams working on the case, she and Matthew headed out with their own list of M Jacksons. By eleven, they'd already met with two men of that name, both dead ends.

One of them was an elderly man in a wheelchair, the other a college student who had numerous alibis for the times of the shootings. So far, the most danger they'd been in was from nearly tripping over all the junk on the student's dorm room floor.

Jay Brady had insisted that every team in search of the Jackson in question be dressed in protective gear, so Charli and Matthew had body armor under their shirts. Of course, Charli would have donned a vest even without the agent's instructions. Potentially encountering an unhinged man with access to a firearm was a recipe for a risky situation, even in protective equipment.

After all, there were plenty of places on her body that wasn't covered in Kevlar.

Matthew offered Charli a fist. "You ready for this?"

She bumped it. "I was born ready."

He didn't laugh or joke back. Despite her weak attempt at humor, adrenaline pulsed through her system. With each step Charli took, her heart pounded in her chest.

Every time they crossed an M Jackson off their list, their chances of meeting *the* M Jackson increased.

The tension could be cut with a knife and served up like a slice of cake. Both she and Matthew had their hands on their firearms while trying to look as casual as possible.

In any situation where a law enforcement officer had to approach a potential criminal, there was the possibility that they were risking their lives. Not long ago, Matthew had been stabbed on the job, but this particular criminal felt especially dangerous. He'd killed so many in a short span of time. If this was indeed their guy, would he try to take out two detectives as a last hurrah?

Charli swallowed hard before pressing her finger to the doorbell, making sure she stepped to the side so that she couldn't be in range if anyone shot through the door. Matthew did the same on the other side.

"I don't think anyone's going to answer." Matthew's words were a whisper in the wind.

When the door jerked open, Charli rested a hand on her firearm, ready to spring into action. In her mind, she pictured M Jackson with hollow brown eyes and a couple horns sprouting from his head.

Instead, she was met with a pair of ocean eyes, which were currently wide in a mix of curiosity and confusion. They were also bloodshot. In fact, the woman before them appeared to have been recently crying.

Charli exchanged a glance with Matthew, anticipation fluttering in her chest. Could this be it?

"May I help you?" Her apple cheeks lifted as she offered a polite smile. When her gaze dropped to their weapons, the smile disappeared. "What do you want?"

Keeping her gaze locked on the empty space behind the woman, Charli smiled a lukewarm greeting. "I'm Detective Cross, and this is my partner, Detective Church." She flashed her badge at the woman. "Is this the Jackson residence?"

She nodded. "Why?"

Charli wished so badly that she had a full name to offer the woman, but it was what it was. "We're attempting to locate a gentleman whose first initial is M."

"Well, my husband's first name is Martin." The woman's worry was palpable with an undercurrent of something else. Fear? "H-he's not here. He left in the middle of eating his breakfast, and he didn't tell me where he was going. Has my husband done something wrong?"

Charli and Matthew exchanged a worried glance.

Despite the pitter-patter in her chest, Charli forced herself to remain calm. They needed answers, and they needed them quickly.

"We don't know yet." Charli nodded a silent communication for Matthew to take a little stroll to the side of the house just in case their suspect was sneaking out, or worse, sneaking up on them. "When did he leave?"

The woman raised a hand to her throat. "I-I don't know. I needed to run to the store for a few minutes, and when I got back, he was gone. So, maybe ten or twenty minutes ago? Please tell me what's going on." When Charli didn't answer right away, her breath quickened. "I've seen the news of that shooter going around town. You don't think Martin had something to do with this, do you?"

"Mrs. Jackson, I—"

The woman shook her head. "It's Mrs. Neeson. Jane Neeson. I didn't take my husband's last name when we married. And please tell me what's going on with my husband. He hasn't been himself lately." She stepped out the front door, her gaze darting up and down the street.

Her name was oddly familiar, but Charli couldn't immediately place it. "Mrs. Neeson, we're conducting an investigation and are currently attempting to gather information. It's critical that you tell us everything you can about your husband's recent behavior."

Jane's face crumpled, and she swiped at a tear trickling down her cheek. "He's been acting so strange lately. He's been angry, and he talks to himself a lot. The way he looks at me…" She shuddered. "Sometimes, I think he hates me. He's not the Martin I know."

Either Jane Neeson was telling the truth, or she was one hell of an actress.

While Jane pulled a tissue from a pocket of her dress, Charli caught Matthew's attention, mouthing for him to call Preston with an update and to ask for another patrol car to be sent their way. Both Ruth and Agent Brady needed to know what they'd learned so far.

"Mrs. Neeson, can you try calling your husband? It's extremely important that we get in touch with him immediately."

The bun on the top of Jane's head flopped as she nodded. "Yes, I'll call him, but he doesn't answer my calls often, not anymore." She pulled her phone out of her dress pocket and dialed on speakerphone, but it went straight to voicemail. "I'm sorry. He doesn't usually answer my calls when he's out. I think he wants space from me. He's been distant and angry lately, like someone has flipped a switch."

Charli flashed the woman an empathetic smile. "Do you think your husband's change in behavior could have anything to do with his health crisis?"

"Health crisis?" Her eyes were frantic, searching for answers. "What do you mean?"

Jane's confusion threw Charli for a loop. "Your husband has been going to the hospital for regular scans, but we aren't sure why. We're still waiting on his records, but we assumed he was ill."

Jane's jaw dropped open. "I could tell Martin has lost weight, and he's acted different, of course, but..." She slapped a hand over her mouth. "Oh no."

Charli watched the woman closely. "Mrs. Neeson? What's wrong?"

She didn't answer right away but took a few steps into the entryway and opened the drawer of a cherry entry table next to the front door. She turned around, holding up a piece of paper.

"Martin got this about a month ago. A bill from a Dr. Grubner." Jane bit her bottom lip. "Martin told me that the bill was a mistake, and that he called the hospital and cleared it up. He said there was another patient named Martin Jackson, and they sent us this invoice by accident. Do you think that's possible? That we got the wrong invoice?" Her eyes filled with desperation. "And maybe this other Martin Jackson is the actual suspect you're looking for. Because my Martin isn't a criminal. He's a good man. He's been acting strange lately, but..."

Charli put a hand on the distraught woman's arm, breaking her own personal no physical contact rule, which was something she'd been doing lately. "Ma'am, does your husband own a Glock 19?"

The color drained from Mrs. Neeson's face, and she dropped the invoice to steady herself against the doorjamb. "No."

Disappointment hit Charli like a punch. "Are you—"

"It's mine." Jane shook her head back and forth as if

attempting to clear her mind. "I mean, it's in my name. I bought it for my husband as a gift."

A piece of the puzzle clicked into position in Charli's mind.

Over the past couple days, Charli had gone over the names of Savannah residents who owned both a Glock 19 and a Honda with a fine-tooth comb. It was too many names to check up on, but Charli had familiarized herself with them in case they popped up again. One of those names was Neeson.

Charli's mouth had gone dry. "And do you own an older model Honda Accord?"

"Well, yes, I…" Jane's hands began to tremble. "Wait, the shooter has a Honda, right? It couldn't be mine, though. Martin had to take it to a garage. He said something was wrong with the transmission."

If that was true, then this M Jackson might not be their man. "Mrs. Neeson, can you tell me the name of the garage?"

Jane frowned. "He usually uses Fred over at Fred's Auto, but he didn't tell me that's where he'd taken it specifically."

Matthew was just stuffing his phone back into his pocket when Charli caught his eye. She waved him over. "Can you make another call? Fred's Auto. See if Martin Jackson dropped off a Honda Accord for service."

To his credit, Matthew didn't even blink. He just pulled his phone back out of his pocket and strolled away again.

"You're not saying…you're not asking me…no." The words tumbled out of Jane's mouth in a rush.

Watching her partner speak into his phone, the seconds seemed eternally slow. When he disconnected the call, he gave her a slight shake of his head.

Charli's pulse picked up speed. "Mrs. Neeson, is there another garage where he might have taken that car?"

Jane just stared at her. Not blinking. Barely breathing.

"Okay...let's get you inside."

Taking the woman's arm, Charli led her through the foyer and into a living room that was a bit too floral for Charli's taste. A glop of something that looked like oatmeal had been spilled on the sofa, so Charli directed the woman into a chair.

"I'll get her some water."

Charli nodded at her partner before squatting before the stricken woman. "I know this is a terrible shock, but I need you to please think, Mrs. Neeson. Not only where that car might be but also where your husband might have gone this morning."

Jane took the glass Matthew handed her.

Giving the woman a few minutes to compose herself, Charli pulled out her cell phone and stepped back into the foyer. There, the hospital bill that Jane had dropped caught her attention. She picked it up. St. George Hospital.

Another puzzle piece shifted, and Charli's mind grew crystal clear.

Martin Jackson was angry at those who he felt let him down. Of all the people in the world who would have let him down the most...

She turned the bill over. Dr. Beauford Grubner. Oncology Department.

Keeping her focus on Jane, she placed a call.

"Special Agent Jay Brady."

Charli didn't bother with a greeting. "I think we found *the* M Jackson's house, but he's not here. Detective Church and I are with his wife. We have a patrol car on its way, so I'm going to ask the officer to stay with her. We need SWAT at St. George Hospital since there is a high likelihood the next target is Dr. Beauford Grubner. He works in oncology. I'll call the security team on our way over. Could you have someone call his office to inform them of the situation?"

Before Charli ended the call, Agent Brady was already barking out orders, and she was thankful to be working with such a competent leader.

But no matter how efficient their team was, would they arrive at the hospital in time to prevent another murder?

31

Charli floored it to the hospital. Really floored it this time. If there was ever a time to make an exception to her internal rule, it was now.

It helped that they were only six minutes from St. George's. With the help of her newly lead foot, they'd hopefully make it there in three.

Matthew was on speaker with hospital security. "No, do not have your security team go toward the office. You will only escalate the situation if the suspect is already there. Start evacuating the other departments closest to oncology. Be as discreet but as quick as possible. Get all your people on this."

The security guard sounded like he was still a kid. His voice shook as he called the other guards. "We need to evacuate everyone we can. Code silver. I repeat, we have a code silver." There was some static from his walkie on the other end of the line. "Okay, what else do I need to do?"

"Our officers need to be aware of all entrances that go into the oncology department. And if any of those entrances are out of view of the oncology lobby, shut them down. But make sure nobody can see you do so."

"This. This is too much. This is my first week. I need my supervisor to call you, okay? He knows the entrances. I don't. He'll call you in one second."

"Wait, man, just—" The kid hung up. "Dammit!" Matthew slammed his fist on the dash before poking a finger at his phone again.

Charli jerked the wheel to make a sharp right turn. "Matt, don't call him back. He won't be any more helpful. Call Brady instead. See if he's gotten in contact with the receptionist in Dr. Grubner's office."

Matthew made the call. "Have you contacted Dr. Grubner or anyone in his offices?"

"No contact with Dr. Grubner. I've reached the receptionist, who I'm now texting. She can't speak out loud because she's got a Martin Jackson sitting in the waiting room waiting for the doctor to return."

Oh no.

Charli had never wanted to be wrong so badly.

"Do we have an entry path yet?"

"When SWAT arrives, they'll be coming in through the south-facing outer entrance. The receptionist has been instructed to make an exit to the bathrooms before our entry. Jackson is the only one in the lobby at this time. If all goes as planned, we can beat Dr. Grubner to the office and take him down."

"Copy that. ETA is…" Matthew glanced up at Charli, who held up one finger, "one minute. We'll arrive before SWAT."

Charli had entered a crime scene with SWAT before, but not with a team that she knew would be this massive. Adrenaline coursed through her veins, her heart threatening to pound right out of her chest. But Charli's mind was clearer than ever.

Despite the stress of the situation, there was relief. They'd found their bad guy, and with that knowledge, they'd be able to stop him. Martin Jackson was waiting in that lobby for Dr. Grubner, completely unaware of the fact that SWAT was waiting outside for him. It ended here. The city would be in terror no more.

When Charli screeched to a halt in the parking lot, the hospital security team had already taped off the areas that led to the oncology suite. A flood of people was being guided away from the hospital, with patients being wheeled out on gurneys and in wheelchairs.

As soon as Charli had shut the car door behind her, a white Mercedes pulled up to the caution tape line. A lanky man with graying hair in a white lab coat popped out of his car and scratched his head. He glanced around, his eyes landing on Charli.

"Hey, what's going on here? I've got to get to my office. Can I just step over this tape or what?"

Step over the tape? Was he really asking that? Civilians could be so oblivious to danger, even when it was right in front of them.

"Sir, nobody is permitted to enter the building. I need you to…" Charli paused when she found the name tag pinned to his lab coat. "Dr. Grubner, I need you to step this way now, please." Charli waved down a police car pulling in. "This is him! We've got Dr. Grubner!"

The doctor was the picture of confusion as he sputtered and tried to pull out of Charli's grip. "You've got me? But why do you need me?"

"Dr. Grubner, there's a man with a gun inside the hospital." When he didn't budge, Charli took it upon herself to gently push him forward. The sooner they had him in the vehicle, the better. Martin could still run out of the office at any moment, guns blazing. "We believe you are the intended victim. I need you to sit in the back seat here until we've got the situation under control."

"Me?" The doctor's voice came out squeaky with shock. "But there must be some mistake. Why would someone want to kill me? Who would—"

"An officer will explain more. Right now, time is of the essence, and we need to apprehend the man in your waiting room."

"But—"

Charli shut the door in the doctor's face and gave the young officer instructions to get him to the end of the parking lot and not let him out of the car for any reason.

"Yes, ma'am."

As she watched them pull away, the doctor's nose pressed to the glass, Matthew handed her an inner-ear microphone. She secured it in place and was immediately privy to all the official chatter going on around her.

"Dr. Grubner is secured," she said into the line.

Brady's voice broke through the chatter. "Copy that. I've got more officers on the way. We have an officer with Jackson's wife, right?"

"Yes, she won't be able to contact him without us knowing."

Charli had seen people do even stupider things.

There was a pause before Brady spoke again. "Copy. We have a problem. The receptionist is reporting that Martin Jackson is acting suspicious. I think she's having trouble holding her composure." A long pause racked at Charli's nerves before Brady came back on the line. "I've just received a text message that the receptionist is heading for the bathroom. She says there's very little cell service in the facilities, so we'll give her two minutes, then SWAT will move in."

The SWAT team was already lining up on the back wall of the building that led to the oncology suite. Charli and

Matthew ran over and huddled with a few who were looking over a map of the building. Several windows gave whoever was inside the lobby a line of sight outside, so when they moved to the entrance, they had to move fast.

The first ten members of the SWAT team held ballistic shields out in front of them, prepared for incoming fire. They would enter first, and Charli and Matthew would follow behind.

Charli's heart pounded in her chest, threatening to explode. Despite the adrenaline that coursed through her veins, a blanket of calm covered her.

Although this plan had come together quickly, Charli had a sense of ease. They had protective gear and an efficient SWAT team, and they were in communication with the receptionist, who knew to get out of the way.

With no hostage to threaten, Charli envisioned a smooth arrest. Even if Martin tried to shoot at the officers, the Kevlar vests and ballistic shields could easily handle rounds from a Glock 19. He'd run out of bullets eventually, and they'd swoop in with the arrest.

It would be damn hard for Martin Jackson to get out of this one. And now that Dr. Grubner was safely in a police vehicle, Charli was confident there would be no more deaths at the hands of this killer.

Don't get ahead of yourself.

Charli shook off the thought, determined not to let anything deter her focus from taking down the man who had terrorized Savannah for the past few days.

Along with several other officers, Charli and Matthew lined up behind the front line of SWAT team. They waited for the commander's instructions in their ear comms.

They didn't have to wait long.

"Units, move into the office, now!"

Stealthy as a lion stalking its prey, the front-line officers rushed toward the oncology lobby. With her weapon pointed to the floor, Charli ran up to the corner wall, Matthew close by her side.

Not making a sound, one of the SWAT members reached for the door handle. It was locked. A few seconds later, shards of glass exploded as a second SWAT member breached the door with a battering ram.

Before the glass could even hit the floor, the team was inside, creating a line of human shields from potential bullets. Then...

A dark silence followed.

A whoosh of air escaped Charli's lungs. She hadn't even realized she'd been holding her breath. She'd been expecting screaming and gunfire, so the absence of those sounds threw her off track.

"Hey, man." The voice in her ear made her jump. "Looks like you're in a bad situation. Put the gun down and let the girl go so we can talk about it."

Oh no.

Sneaking a peek between the shields, Charli's heart fell.

Martin Jackson was sitting behind a petite blonde woman. She cried silently while Martin pressed a gun to her neck.

The receptionist hadn't been able to get away after all.

This was bad. One wrong move could result in the receptionist's head being blown to bits. The only movement in Charli's body was the rise and fall of her chest.

This wasn't what was supposed to happen. They'd been given the go-ahead to breach the door because the receptionist was heading to the bathroom. He wasn't supposed to be able to hurt anyone else.

Get over it. Focus on the problem in front of you.

Physically, Martin Jackson was a mess. Gaunt to the point of skeletal, his skin had a yellow tinge. As frail as he appeared, there was a sinister gleam in his eyes that Charli could only describe as unhinged.

"I'm happy to talk!" Martin's laugh was on the verge of being maniacal. "Let's talk about Dr. Grubner. Where is he? I know he should be here by now, as this pretty little lady happily told me not long ago."

"Why don't you put down your weapon and we'll talk about Dr. Grubner." The SWAT team leader's voice was calm to the point of soothing.

Martin's cheeks went fire red. "Where is he?" His voice was a roar, like a predator who had missed his prey. He wasn't unlike a lion, lamenting the gazelle that had escaped his grasp.

For the next few minutes, the team leader attempted to de-escalate the situation, but he hadn't been privy to the cards Martin Jackson had written. He hadn't spoken to his wife.

Charli had.

Though she'd received the standard hostage negotiation training, she didn't have the proper skills to serve as a proper negotiator. She did have one advantage...she knew this man's mind. Could she do it, though? She hadn't mentally prepared herself for an incident quite like this.

No time like the present.

She took a deep breath and stepped forward, moving behind one of the shields of a front-line SWAT member. One of Charli's hands gripped the shield, and the SWAT member allowed her to take it with her.

"Hi, Mr. Jackson. I'm Detective Charli Cross. I've just come from your house after speaking to your wife, and she's very worried about you."

There was a wicked gleam in Jackson's eyes. "I don't give a shit about my wife."

That went over well.

"It seems to me that you're angry with the people who tried to help you with your cancer."

A mirthless laugh erupted, and their suspect stared at Charli with cold, dead eyes. "Help me? They killed me."

"How did they kill you?" Charli spoke in an even tone.

Jackson's left hand shook as he held the gun to the receptionist's head, and Charli caught a glimpse of his right hand wrapped up in a bandage.

"You have no idea what I've been through. This bastard of a doctor told me that my disease was terminal without batting an eyelash. And that bitch who called herself a therapist fed me useless platitudes. She told me to feel my feelings. Gave me hope that I'd be cured." His face contorted with a mixture of rage and sadness and fear that tugged at Charli's heart. "Can you believe that? No one understands. No one!"

Just keep him talking. Stay calm, Charli. You've got this.

"It seems to me that you feel they peddled lies to you."

He scoffed. "You're damn right they did."

Charli took in another calming breath. "I can see how their words were just a bunch of shit to you."

Jackson laughed, turning from lion to hyena. "Don't condescend to me. Look, I know I'm going to jail. We both know I killed enough people to be put away for life." Another scoff. "Or whatever the rest of my life is going to be. But before I go, I'm taking one more with me. It can be Dr. Grubner's or this receptionist's. Your call." His grin went from ear to ear now, but the rest of his body remained unmoving.

Tears streamed down the young woman's cheeks like a waterfall. Her blonde hair was crinkling where the gun pressed against her.

With tension rising by the second, Charli tapped into everything she'd learned about hostage negotiations. She knew she had to be empathetic with this man. And as much as she wanted to hate him for murdering innocent people, she could tell he was hurting and confused, and there was a part of her that didn't have to pretend to empathize.

"Why do you want to hurt Dr. Grubner? You seem like a smart man, a rational man, so I assume you have a good reason for it." Charli was inching forward with the shield, her gun still in her other hand.

Jackson shrugged. "You're here. You must know. You got me figured out, right? We're at the hospital. I assume you've seized my medical records and know about the pancreatic cancer."

Actually, Charli didn't. Those records hadn't yet come in. But it wouldn't help to say as much. "I'm so sorry, Mr. Jackson. You don't deserve that."

Martin's laugh was more sarcastic this time. "That's what Damian says."

Who the hell? "Who's Damian?"

One side of his mouth lifted. "My cancer. The therapist bitch told me that I should name it, talk to it." The smile slid away, and the crazy eyes returned. "I did, and do you know what?"

"What?"

"The cancer talked back."

A shiver walked up Charli's spine. "What did the cancer tell you?"

"Damian told me that Dr. Grubner didn't do enough. It's his job to catch the cancer. When he told me how bad it was, it was like he was telling me what he had for lunch." The gun shook in Jackson's hand, but it never shifted from the receptionist's head as she choked out quiet sobs.

Charli took another step closer.

"What about the others? How did they fail you?"

Jackson's nostrils flared. "I didn't deserve the false hope and promises those people gave me. Didn't deserve my x-ray technician to refer me to Cornerstone. Didn't deserve to meet the pastor there, who put me in Haley's worthless grief group. Definitely didn't deserve to hear that asshole mini-mart owner tell me in grief group that it would all be okay because his cancer went into remission just fine. And they all got what they deserved." Jackson closed his eyes before taking a long breath. "But nobody deserves it more than Dr. Grubner."

How was Charli going to spin this? She had to empathize with this man, but if she took it too far, he'd recognize her words as fake, and that could escalate the situation. Hostage negotiating was a dangerous game.

"I think I understand now. You believe Dr. Grubner deserves to die because he so casually diagnosed you. But what has his receptionist done? You're not a monster, Mr. Jackson. You're not going to take her life for no reason, right?"

Jackson lifted his chin and glared at Charli. "Look at her. She has a perfectly healthy body, but do you think that's good enough?" He shifted the gun from the woman's temple to her overly inflated lips. "No. She not only takes her good health for granted, she has people shoot poison under her skin so she can look like a trout."

For the first time, Charli saw something besides fear in the receptionist's eyes. The remark had pissed her off.

Charli ignored her and focused on the man with the gun. There was a twang of real pain in his voice, not just anger. But hurt. Under this aggressive madman, there was a man who was terrified of dying. And he didn't understand why cancer had chosen him instead of so many others.

"That's good," a voice whispered in her ear. "Keep him talking. If you can get him to move the gun away, we'll take the shot."

Charli shivered at the reminder of how many sharpshooters were standing behind her. She was just glad they were on her side.

Martin's eyebrows lifted. "How about a trade? Her for Dr. Grubner. That's the only thing that will end this."

No way in hell could she do that, but she needed to keep him talking. "How do you suggest I convince Dr. Grubner to trade places with that young woman?"

Jackson seemed as stumped as she felt, then he smiled. "Not my problem."

She smiled right back. "I think it is. You're in a no-win situation, Mr. Jackson. Is this the legacy you want to leave?"

The gunman growled before raising his voice. "What legacy did I have to begin with? I was just some shmuck doing what the world told him to do. Get married. Get a job. Jane and I couldn't even have kids, so there's not even anyone who'll miss me. At least now, someone will remember my name."

How the hell was she supposed to argue with that?

"That's very sad, Mr. Jackson. I'm so sorry you feel that way."

Charli was coming to a truth she'd never say out loud.

If Martin Jackson was determined to kill one more person, Charli wasn't going to talk him out of it. She needed another tactic, a distraction. The more time that passed, the more certain she was that this standoff wasn't going to end without violence.

She thought about his letters and pulled out one of the lines. "Penny for your thoughts."

Instead of getting pissed off enough to point the gun at Charli like she'd hoped, he grinned. "You understood the token?"

"Yeah. Is Dr. Grubner supposed to get your last penny?" She held out a hand. "I'll give it to him if you want."

Jackson laughed, though the sound didn't last as long as

she would have preferred. "You're funny. I bet you'd do a much better job of telling people they were going to die than Grubner."

Inspiration struck. "How do you wish he would have told you?" Charli nodded at the receptionist. "Can you show me with her?"

Charli could tell that he'd never considered the question because nearly a full minute ticked by while he thought it through. Finally, he met her gaze. "I don't know, but I sure would have done a better job than Grubner did."

Charli lifted a shoulder. "You think? Right now, you've got a young woman's life in your hands, and you've been pretty callus in talking about her death to her." She licked her lips. "I have an idea. How much time do you have left?"

Pain twisted his features. "About a month."

"How about, instead of continuing to kill, you teach doctors and therapists what you needed to hear? During this month, just think of the difference you can make for others. That's a real legacy."

Was she getting through to him? She couldn't tell. His face had relaxed into a blank mask.

When he laughed, Charli's shoulders fell. Where was the fucking hostage negotiator? She was clearly no good at this.

"Do you really think I'm that stupid? If I put this gun down, I'll never get the chance to do anything but rot in a cell."

Charli shook her head. "That's not true. I'll personally make sure of it."

Jackson narrowed his eyes at her. "I want to tell Dr. Grubner how I feel face to face, right now. Can you person-ally make sure that happens too?"

Think. Think. Think.

"I can't force Dr. Grubner to come in here, but..." Charli raised a finger, "maybe you can."

Jackson's eyes popped open in surprise. His body inched forward, his grasp on the receptionist tightening. "Excuse me?"

As much as she didn't want to, Charli slid her gun into her holster. With that hand, she pulled out her phone. "Give Dr. Grubner a chance to do the right thing. Tell him he can man up and come in here to save his receptionist's life, or she can die. It's up to him." Charli began tapping the screen randomly. "I've dialed his number for you. Want it?"

Before giving him a chance to answer, she tossed her phone in his direction, praying she was doing the right thing.

With the left hand holding the gun and his right one bandaged, panic flashed across Jackson's face, his indecision evident. Charli could only hope his hatred of the oncologist and his desire for revenge would at the very least cause him to lower the weapon.

It did.

"Get down!"

Charli's command was barely out of her mouth before a shot came from behind her. Blood exploded from Jackson's shoulder, painting the white wall behind him.

Screeching like a dying animal, Jackson flailed as the receptionist dropped to the floor so fast, her body was a blur. Before Charli could even shout out additional instructions, she was rolling like a tornado toward the SWAT team. It was the absolute perfect move.

A second shot penetrated Jackson's chest, and the man fell to his knees. Shock made his facial features slack, but his dark eyes continued to burn his hate.

Charli lunged for his gun, her hand closing over the cold steel.

"Bitch." Even as injured as he was, Jackson wasn't willing to let the Glock go. Fueled by adrenaline and hate, he attempted to turn the weapon on her. "Penny...for...your... thoughts..." His spittle sprayed her face with each word.

Rage went through her, and Charli managed to get the barrel turned to the floor before the weapon exploded. Ears ringing, Charli lifted a knee and centered Jackson's balls. The second his grip loosened, she managed to tug the gun free just before the SWAT team closed in.

Breathing hard, Charli took a few steps back and didn't even blink as someone slid the Glock out of her hand.

They'd done it.

Martin Jackson's three-day reign of terror was over.

32

Matthew's gaze drifted to where Ruth and Agent Brady were rendezvousing in the hospital parking lot next to a collection of squad cars. By the time Martin Jackson had been taken down, the sergeant and the lead FBI agent had arrived on the scene.

Irony of ironies, the dying man had been rushed into surgery to treat the bullet wounds to his chest and shoulder. Last Matthew heard, Jackson's chances were good for a full recovery from his wounds.

He'd be healed just before he died.

Relief washed over Matthew as Charli stepped out of the hospital, and he shook off the exhaustion that had set in from the long days and grueling nights he'd spent on this case. Tonight, he wasn't going to get woken up in the wee hours of the morning to the news that another innocent citizen had been shot in the street. The stress of this case had been eating away at him with each passing day.

Charli came straight to him, and it took everything inside him not to pull her in for a great big hug. Instead, he held out a fist and smiled as she bumped it with hers.

"You scared me in there, you know?" He still couldn't believe she'd put her gun away while only a few yards from that maniac.

She rubbed the back of her neck. "Scared myself a little bit too, truth be told." She glanced past his shoulder. "Look sharp. The bosses are on their way."

Matthew turned to find Ruth and Agent Brady almost upon them. The sergeant spoke first. "What happened in there?"

Still looking a little dazed, Charli seemed to search for the right words, but Matthew beat her to it. "For starters, Detective Cross was a rock star."

Wait. Was that a smile on Brady's face? Matthew did a double take.

Brady was still grinning as he nodded. "I heard."

Ruth looked annoyed. "I'd like to hear too."

After Matthew spent a couple minutes reliving the scene for their boss, Ruth's annoyance faded to impressed.

She stuck out a hand, and Charli shook it. "Nice job, Detective Cross. Excellent work, both of you." Her expression turned serious. "Who discharged Jackson's weapon?"

Charli frowned. "What do you mean?"

"Since both you and Jackson were wrestling for the weapon, do you know who actually pulled the trigger?"

Matthew couldn't believe the sergeant was even asking the question, but since Charli wasn't answering, he would. "Jackson, of course."

But Charli was staring out into space. "Honestly, I'm not sure. I think his finger was on the trigger, but I might have forced him to pull it." She shook her head, honest to a fault. "I just don't know."

Ruth sighed. "To cover all our bases, I'm going to put you on paid administrative leave while it's all sorted out."

His partner nodded, stuffing her hands into her pockets. "I understand."

Charli knew as well as Matthew did that an officer-involved shooting meant an investigation would ensue, but he didn't miss the hint of disappointment on her face.

"Would you look at that?" Matthew winked at Charli. "You take down the killer, and then you get to take a paid vacation and leave me with all the paperwork."

Charli rolled her eyes, throwing him a playful punch in the shoulder. "Vacation, ha! I'll be under a mountain of paperwork myself, going to mandatory counseling, and all that fun stuff, as you well know."

Brady cleared his throat, a hint of a smile still on his face. It seemed foreign on the man who was normally all business. "I want to commend you both on your work here. We never would have reached this point this fast without you. You two both are fantastic detectives, and while I hope it's a good long while before a case brings me back to Savannah, it would be an honor to work with you two again. Now, if you'll excuse me, I need to speak with my team." Brady was already walking away before either of them could answer.

Ruth squeezed Charli's arm. "Go enjoy a couple days off."

Charli scowled. "I guess I'll psych myself up for some mandatory counseling."

Ruth placed a hand on her hip, a roguish gleam in her eye. "Of course, if you'd rather work, you can always stand in for me at the press conference. I know how much you love to be on camera."

Charli threw up both hands and backed away. "That's okay. With the media camped out at the precinct, I think I've had enough cameras flashed in my face to last me a good long while."

"I thought as much. I'll get your mandatory counseling scheduled immediately, and you've got a bit of paperwork to fill out, but try to treat the next few days like a vacation, Detective Cross. Lord knows you've earned it." Concern flashed across the sergeant's face. "And since we're already at the hospital, it wouldn't hurt for you to get checked out. How are you holding up mentally?"

Charli lifted her chin, looking almost insulted. "I'm fine. We caught the bad guy."

Ruth wagged a finger. "And you almost got your head blown off in the process." With that cheery reminder, the sergeant walked away.

Matthew put a hand on Charli's shoulder. "You really do deserve a break. You were awesome in there, and you've been working nonstop. The stress of these back-to-back cases has got to be getting to you because I know I'm exhausted."

Charli tapped the pavement with the toe of her boot, and he could tell she was working up to a confession. "It's not even just work. Ever since I got those letters about Madeline, she's been on my mind. And not just her, but I've been thinking about her killer. Unless someone is just trying to screw with me, he could still be out there. I've tried to throw myself into work and shove all these thoughts aside, but they always return." She ran a hand under her nose. "And now that I'll be off a couple days, I'll have plenty of time on my hands to do nothing but think."

A pang went through Matthew's chest. He hated seeing his partner so despondent, but there was little he could do to comfort her. "Maybe that's a good thing, Charli. Maybe you gotta face this head-on. You've got some time to think about it now, and you'll be talking with a counselor." He turned her until she faced him straight on. "Speak to them about Madeline, okay? You've held a lot of things inside for a long time."

Charli shrugged, her gaze falling to the ground. "Yeah, maybe I will."

Before Matthew could say anything else, Preston Powell's

voice rang out behind him. "Hey, I just heard what you did!" Powell jogged toward them, his hand raised for a high five.

Charli slapped his palm, a grin spreading across her face. "It was a team effort. I'm just glad we got that bastard."

"Are you kidding me? The SWAT guy I spoke to said you were better than some of the negotiators on staff. Excellent work. Savannah is safe tonight because of you." His eyes twinkled as he stared at her.

Give me a break.

Matthew resisted the urge to fake gag in front of his colleagues. But if he were being honest with himself, Preston Powell was growing on him, little by little.

Since they'd first worked a case together, Matthew had sensed the GBI agent had feelings for Charli, which instantly put the guy on his radar. Charli didn't have any brothers, but Matthew would sure as hell do his best to protect her like she was his little sis. They were more than just partners. They were family.

And the more he heard Preston talk to Charli, the more Matthew started to think he was a good guy. Matthew had met plenty of asshole government agents who wouldn't be able to celebrate someone else's win on the case, but he was happy that Preston wasn't that way.

"Well, thank you. I appreciate it." Charli's smile was almost as big as Preston's. Although she'd denied any attraction to the agent, Matthew wasn't so sure.

"Of course. And I also hear you're on leave. If you're bored in the next few days and wanna get lunch with a friend, I'm around." Preston ran his fingers through the side of his hair.

Almost mirroring him, Charli tucked her own short hair behind her ear. "Yeah, I might take you up on that."

When another agent pulled Preston away from them, Matthew couldn't resist the opportunity to tease his partner.

"Lunch with a friend, huh?" Matthew nudged her shoulder, giving her a dramatic wink.

"Yes!" Charli pushed him back, harder than he'd nudged her by a lot. "It's possible for a man and woman to be just friends. What do you think you and I are?"

Matthew couldn't help but smile because Charli really was his best friend. She had his back like nobody else, and he could call her with any problem, whether it was day or night. Not that he needed to.

Lately, they'd spent every waking moment together and had worked into the wee hours of the morning on some of their cases. "Yeah, well, it's a little harder to be just friends with a guy who is staring at you with googly eyes. But if you need a real *friend* during your mandatory vacation, call me."

"Of course I will, but don't expect to have a lot of free time yourself. I think Ruth will be on you like white on rice." She shot him an exaggerated wink. "Or Janice. Stay out of trouble without me."

Ugh...Janice. He didn't think so.

He flipped Charli off. "You know I won't."

33

The beer Rebecca handed Charli was icy cold in her hand. She hadn't planned to drink, but her friend had come over bearing gifts, so she obliged. Just one beer wouldn't hurt.

"Honestly, Charli, I think you need to take some time off work more often. I've had so much fun with you the last few evenings."

Pushing Madeline out of her head had been more difficult than Charli had expected. Without her job keeping her occupied, Madeline was hiding behind every corner. For the first two days, it drove Charli mad.

She had taken both Preston and Matthew up on their offers to hang out, having eaten lunch with Preston yesterday and Matthew the day before. They were still working, though, and hadn't had much time to spare. Rebecca, on the other hand, had come over every evening after work.

Spending time with her high school friend was just what she needed to lift her spirits and put life in perspective. They'd spent some time reflecting on memories of Madeline, which Charli worried would increase her obsession, but it actually seemed to help. Perhaps Matthew was right about facing this thing head-on.

Charli still hadn't brought up Madeline in her counseling sessions, though. Speaking about her to a complete stranger was just...weird.

"So, I saw the shooter is recovering just fine." Rebecca cracked the top of her beer open with a bottle opener on her key chain. The quick motion made her voluminous hair bounce around her shoulders.

Although Charli had been aware of this already, she hadn't been able to share details of the case with her friend. When he no longer needed to heal in the hospital, he would be taken into custody. Matthew kept her up to date on the case, though it was pretty cut and dry.

They'd found no evidence that the wife had been involved, other than the fact that the Honda and Glock were in her name. That didn't surprise Charli one bit. Not only had her shock appeared genuine, but she was extremely cooperative with the police.

"Yep. He's going to be just fine until he dies in a couple weeks." The last few words came out more solemn than Charli intended.

As much tragedy as the man had caused, Charli couldn't bring herself to hate Martin Jackson. He clearly hadn't been in his right mind. With his recently diagnosed terminal pancreatic cancer, he'd become aggressive, confused, and angry. As his wife had told them, he had become a completely different man.

Damian.

The fact that he'd had conversations with his cancer was creepy as hell.

"You're such a badass, Charli. Seriously, I don't know how you deal with these situations. I find out I'm late on my gas bill, and the whole world falls apart." Rebecca waved her arm in the air, causing a little bit of beer to splash out of her bottle and fall onto Charli's porch.

Charli chuckled. "I bet if you were actually in these situations, you'd surprise yourself. I never thought I could handle it before either. But then, when people's lives are on the line, you somehow just snap into action. I can't really explain it."

Rebecca smiled and widened her eyes. For every sentence that came out of her mouth, Rebecca had a facial expression for it. "Well, I can. Like I said, you're just a badass."

Before Charli could argue further, her phone rang in her pocket. She wasn't expecting the name on the caller ID.

"Oh, it's my dad." Charli glanced up at Rebecca to gauge her reaction.

"Take it!" Rebecca stood, smoothing out her flowy navy dress as she did. "I should get going, anyway. But we're on for a movie tomorrow night, right?"

"Definitely! Well, assuming work isn't insane tomorrow." This was the last day of Charli's leave, and although she didn't expect her first day back at work to be too hectic, there was no way to know what her day would be like.

"See you then! Just let me know if something changes." Rebecca picked her matching blue purse off Charli's patio table before heading to her car.

Charli picked up the call. "Hello?"

"Hey, guess who I just saw on the news?"

With her dad, Charli could never predict whether he was going to be proud of her actions or complain about the intensity of her job.

"Yeah. That was a crazy one, huh?" Charli tipped her beer back, letting the hops rush down her throat. Rebecca was gone, so she wasn't obligated to drink it, but a little alcohol couldn't hurt as she talked to her dad.

"I gotta admit, Charli, I worry about you. And hearing what you did with that shooter, well, it made me realize we've gone too long without seeing each other. Can we do lunch or dinner next weekend?"

Although Charli hated arguing about her job, she couldn't fault her father for his concern. Hell, even she'd been pretty concerned about this last case. And the time off only gave her more time to analyze what a dangerous situation she'd thrust herself into.

"Sure, Dad. Can you do Sunday evening?"

"Absolutely. Our usual spot?"

"Sounds good to me."

Their conversation was cut short when Charli's phone beeped with another incoming call. As much as she loved her dad, she thanked her lucky stars when Ruth's name flashed across the screen.

"I gotta go, Dad. I'm getting another call, but I'll talk to you soon." Charli hung up with him and quickly switched gears. "Detective Cross."

"Enjoying your vacation?" Although Ruth was probably expecting her to say no, Charli had enjoyed the time away from the precinct. She'd gotten to visit with Rebecca, catch up on sleep, and she'd even made a homecooked meal. Charli couldn't remember the last time she'd eaten something other than fast food or a frozen dinner.

If this time away from work had given Charli any insight into her life, it was that she needed to spend the time she had with loved ones. Her bond with her dad had come secondary to her career for a while, as most things did. She really needed to make working on her relationship with her father more of a priority. He may not always approve of her choices, but he was the only parent she had left.

Charli sighed. After a few days away from the station, she was indeed ready to return to work.

"It hasn't been as bad as I thought." Charli took another sip of her beer, savoring the flavors on her tongue.

"Well, I hope you enjoyed it while it lasted because you're cleared to return to work." She made a sound that was more snort than laughter. "Actually, you were cleared on Friday, but I figured a couple more days wouldn't hurt since it was the weekend. Unfortunately, I need you now."

Charli stiffened. "What's going on?"

"Two teenagers were found in a local park. I've already got Matthew on his way there. When can you leave?"

Thank goodness she'd only had one drink, and only part of it at that. She was still good to drive, and the rush of a new case had her already on her feet.

"Just tell me where, and I'm on my way."

34

W atching her sip beer on her front porch, it was easy for him to remember a time when she was too young to even drink. He couldn't believe he'd been watching her this long without ever making a move.

He glanced down at the newspaper article he'd just read about the good detective's heroism. Pride swelled in his heart, but that wasn't the only thing that began to swell. He shifted in his seat, attempting to make himself more comfortable.

Would Madeline have turned out to be such a fine, upstanding citizen if he'd let her live instead of her friend? He doubted it. With her obsession with boys and looking pretty, she probably would have squandered her life away.

When he'd taken her instead of Charli all those years ago, he'd made the right choice. But he couldn't help but wonder what the prude little teen would have been like. Would she have been as mouthy as Madeline? As terrified? As...satisfying?

He pulled the lock of Madeline's hair out of his pocket,

caressing it with his fingers as his mind drifted to the day he'd made her his.

"Don't touch me! Get your filthy hands off me!"

Even after she'd spent hours gagged and bound, the little devil was still so full of vitality. Nothing got him hard quite like when they fought back...when they struggled.

"You've been a very bad girl, Madeline. Do you know what happens to bad girls like you?"

She spit in his face. "Go to hell."

"Ah, now you're on the right track. Eventually, they do go to hell, but first, they get punished."

Mmm...the events of that day were still vivid in his mind, and he savored every delicious memory. The only thing he'd found as entertaining as finding a new toy to play with was playing with Charlotte Cross's mind over the recent months.

Had he driven her as crazy as she'd driven him? When he woke up every morning, she was the first thing on his mind, and as he drifted off to sleep each night, she was part of his wildest fantasies.

Had the detective gone mad trying to figure out who he was? He'd left her a few clues, and he couldn't wait to see if she'd be able to sniff him out.

His cock was throbbing now, standing at full attention. After all, it wasn't the kill that made his dick hard. It was the foreplay, the anticipation.

Though his fingers itched to close around her pretty little neck, he couldn't kill her. Not yet.

First, he wanted to see if he could knock Charli Cross off her perfect little pedestal.

The End
To be continued...

Thank you for reading.

All of the *Charli Cross Series* books can be found on Amazon.

ACKNOWLEDGMENTS

How does one properly thank everyone involved in taking a dream and making it a reality? Here goes.

In addition to our families, whose unending support provided the foundation for us to find the time and energy to put these thoughts on paper, we want to thank the editors who polished our words and made them shine.

Many thanks to our publisher for risking taking on two newbies and giving us the confidence to become bona fide authors.

More than anyone, we want to thank you, our readers, for clicking on a couple of nobodies and sharing your most important asset, your time, with this book. We hope with all our hearts we made it worthwhile.

Much love,
Mary & Donna

ABOUT THE AUTHOR

Mary Stone

Mary Stone lives among the majestic Blue Ridge Mountains of East Tennessee with her two dogs, four cats, a couple of energetic boys, and a very patient husband.

As a young girl, she would go to bed every night, wondering what type of creature might be lurking underneath. It wasn't until she was older that she learned that the creatures she needed to most fear were human.

Today, she creates vivid stories with courageous, strong heroines and dastardly villains. She invites you to enter her world of serial killers, FBI agents but never damsels in distress. Her female characters can handle themselves, going toe-to-toe with any male character, protagonist or antagonist.

Discover more about Mary Stone on her website.
www.authormarystone.com

Donna Berdel

Raised as an Army brat, Donna has lived all over the world, but no place has given her as much peace as the home she lives in with her husband near Myrtle Beach. But while she now keeps her feet planted firmly in the sand, her mind goes back to those cities and the people she met and said goodbye to so many times.

With her two adopted cats fighting for lap space, she brings those she loved (and those she didn't) back as characters in her books. And yes, it's kind of fun to kill off anyone who was mean to her in the past. Mean clerk at the grocery store...beware!

Connect with Mary Online

facebook.com/authormarystone

goodreads.com/AuthorMaryStone

bookbub.com/profile/3378576590

pinterest.com/MaryStoneAuthor